"Did

Dylan droppe[...]
and began to [...]
know what I saw."

"Did you see into the future?" Sonia asked.

His smile broke into a grin. "I saw a colorful room—white furniture, reds and yellows, a bright blue carpet."

"My bedroom," Sonia said with wonder. "Is that all?"

"No. On the bed . . . look, I don't want to embarrass you."

Did he think she'd be embarrassed by the big Raggedy Ann doll? "Go on. Not much shocks me."

"This might."

"What is it?"

"On the bed I saw you and me . . . making love."

Dear Reader,

When two people fall in love, the world is suddenly new and exciting, and it's that same excitement we bring to you in Silhouette Intimate Moments. These are stories with scope, with grandeur. These characters lead the lives we all dream of, and everything they do reflects the wonder of being in love.

Longer and more sensuous than most romances, Silhouette Intimate Moments novels take you away from everyday life and let you share the magic of love. Adventure, glamour, drama, even suspense—these are the passwords that let you into a world where love has a power beyond the ordinary, where the best authors in the field today create stories of love and commitment that will stay with you always.

In coming months look for novels by your favorite authors: Maura Seger, Parris Afton Bonds, Elizabeth Lowell and Erin St. Claire, to name just a few. And whenever you buy books, look for all the Silhouette Intimate Moments, love stories *for* today's women *by* today's women.

Leslie J. Wainger
Senior Editor
Silhouette Books

IMRL-7/85

Head Over Heels

Sue Ellen Cole

Silhouette Intimate Moments

Published by Silhouette Books New York

America's Publisher of Contemporary Romance

SILHOUETTE BOOKS
300 E. 42nd St., New York, N.Y. 10017

Copyright © 1985 by Sue Ellen Cole

Distributed by Pocket Books

ISBN: 0-373-07103-5

First Silhouette Books printing July, 1985

10 9 8 7 6 5 4 3 2 1

America's Publisher of Contemporary Romance

Printed in the U.S.A.

Chapter 1

THERE WAS A DARK DRAMA ABOUT HIM THAT intrigued her. As he walked through the double glass doors, their eyes met briefly and she was startled by the brilliant turquoise color of his, accented by black lashes and eyebrows.

He gave her a lightning appraisal. Whatever the assessment, his hard, sculpted face revealed nothing; yet she was left feeling oddly vulnerable.

He was well over six feet, and though his broad shoulders were relaxed there was a trace of tension in the rugged line of his jaw. Probably his first time here, thought Sonia. People generally approached the University Psychiatric Hospital with a sense of foreboding, as though it were a hostile jungle teaming with crazed lunatics leaping and screaming down the corridors, chased by harried attendants in white coats.

She watched him glance down with detached amusement at the toys scattered on the floor— dolls with scraggly hair, some naked, limbs twisted and broken; Tonka trucks overturned. It suddenly struck Sonia that the waiting area floor looked like a child's version of the aftermath of war.

Headed in the same direction, she followed him through the double doors and down the hall. The two-toned yellow walls of the narrow corridors suddenly seemed garish and inexplicably neurotic.

With the same detached amusement, he glanced up at the signs over the office doors, signposts to exotic kingdoms.

Behaviorial Medicine.

Eating Disorders Clinic.

Adult Psychiatry Program.

Neurology Clinic.

They turned a corner and both entered a crowded elevator. Suddenly she found herself standing beside him.

He had that tightly coiled shot-out-of-a-cannon look of an actor. Pacino? Stallone? Sonia went to the movies so seldom she wouldn't have known one from the other. But if he were famous, it would have been evident by now. She'd never seen it fail. People in Los Angeles might brag about a blasé attitude toward movie stars, but face-to-face with a live one, they begged an autograph faster than any wide-eyed innocent from Ohio.

He held the elevator door for her at floor B and their eyes met again for a moment. She smiled a brief thank-you and passed him to turn down the hall to her office. A prickly sensation at the back of her neck told her he wasn't far behind.

Having spent the last few years studying what people called "gut feelings," she was intensely aware of her own. A strong emotion like fear churned in her chest. Was it the predatory way he moved, with his confident, long-legged stride, that made her feel she was being stalked?

With some relief she reached the cluster of offices she shared with two other psychologists. Evidently everyone was out to lunch, including the receptionist.

As she checked the messages in her box, she heard the door open behind her.

"I thought it might be you." There was a slight drawl in the low, resonant voice.

She stiffened, knowing who it was without even turning. "You thought what might be me?"

"You're Dr. Barnes?"

"Yes."

She took a deep breath and turned to face him. Damn! Gut feelings were one thing, but this was just the sort of irrational, nervous reaction she had trained herself to suppress. After all, she had dealt with severely disturbed patients in the wards upstairs. This man might give her the impression he had something volatile seething just under the surface, but at the moment the lid was still tightly in place.

His eyelids dropped, slightly shading the intensity of the turquoise eyes. He was sizing her up again, just as he had in the hall, though this time she felt like a bull who was watching a matador ready his sword for the final plunge between the shoulder blades.

He stretched his hand out. "How do you do, Dr. Barnes. My name is Dylan Hamlin."

"Pleased to meet you."

His grip was firm, the large hand warm. Something quite pleasant stirred in her lower regions. Ignoring it, she forced a professional tone. "May I help you with something, Mr. Hamlin?"

"Maybe. I understand you deal in spooks, soothsayers, poltergeists, that sort of thing."

"You make it sound as though I might also deal in hot car stereos."

"Do you?"

"Only if they're inhabited by evil spirits," she said dryly.

He broke into a grin. The tension between them was temporarily in abeyance.

"What is it exactly that you do?"

It was time for her standard demystifying speech. "First of all, I'm a medical psychologist. I see patients here at the hospital. That accounts for a third of my time. Teaching takes up another third. I'm a professor of psychology at the University of Los Angeles. The last third of my job is devoted to independent research. The field I've chosen is parapsychology, which includes some of the things you mentioned—psychic phenomena, ESP, poltergeists, auras, spooks, soothsayers. I'm simply looking into these things in a rational, scientific way."

"Isn't it a rather odd pursuit for a doctor of psychology? I thought you people just ran rats through mazes."

She decided to ignore the insult. Too often she'd felt the same way about the rat psychologists. "Psychical research is going on at various universities all over the world. There are even rumors the Pentagon is involved."

His dark eyebrows rose in amusement. "Having spent some time in the army, I'd say they have enough trouble without grappling with ghosts."

"ESP could be very useful to them," said Sonia. "Imagine being able to send coded messages without radios or telephones."

"I suppose it could eventually cut down their phone bills," he acknowledged. "Heaven knows they waste enough of the taxpayers' money with all those costly overruns on fighter-bombers and cruise missiles."

She smiled. "You see? The practical applications of my work are endless. Now, what can I do for you, Mr. Hamlin?"

He turned serious and slightly hesitant. "I want to talk to you about . . . the psychic research."

"I have a few minutes. Why don't you take a seat in my office. It's the cluttered one on the left. I'll be right in. Would you care for some coffee?"

"That would be very kind. I take it black."

The drawl was even more pronounced with the last phrase and led her to suspect a Southern gentleman lurking under the panther's surface.

As she poured the coffee, she watched him lower his tall, athletic frame into a chair and glance around her office.

She'd often thought the state of her office was a good reflection of the interior of her brain—piled high with bits and pieces of unrelated information. The disparaging remarks from colleagues about her lack of tidiness didn't bother her. She left the meticulous labs and offices to those who dealt with the scurrying little rodents and their mazes.

He would learn nothing about her from the office walls. She purposely hung no framed photographs of family, friends or pets, no revealing paintings, only framed academic certificates. Those curious reporters who expected a psychic researcher's office to replicate a gypsy tent with crystal balls and Tarot card posters were sorely disappointed.

Only in her appearance did she live up to their expectations of a woman who "dealt in spooks and poltergeists." Sonia Barnes had lush, straight black hair and ebony eyes, with high cheekbones inherited from her Romanian mother. Her features had such striking potential that she did everything she could to play them down, including muted lipsticks and drab business suits. Early in her career she had learned the hard lesson that striking beauty works against a woman in the academic community. Other women resented you, and men refused to take you seriously.

So she confined the flamboyant side of her

personality to her private hours. It was a sacrifice; she loved bright colors and outlandish clothes. But the prestigious position at the University of Los Angeles was worth the effort of looking bookish. After all, she rationalized, if actors dressed for roles, why shouldn't people in everyday life?

Sonia set the coffee mugs carefully on the desk and settled into her roomy chair.

He took a sip of the hot liquid and frowned.

"Too strong?" she asked.

"Too hot." He placed the mug back on the desk and regarded her steadily.

She sensed that whatever he wanted to say would not come easily, so she decided to be direct. "Why are you here?"

"I'm psychic."

It was not unusual for people to come into her office with that pronouncement. Ever since the *L.A. Times* article she had been besieged by everyone from witches with conical hats to toga-toting soothsayers who claimed to read the future from casting leftover Kentucky Fried Chicken bones. Sonia firmly turned away these costumed crazies. It was difficult enough bucking the psychology establishment at a conservative university for budgets and lab space. She didn't need the added onus of these Hollywood crazy types traipsing through the hospital brandishing their magic wands.

"Are you here to volunteer for one of my lab experiments?"

"No." He took the coffee mug again and this

time drank from it. "I want you to get rid of my psychic ability for me."

"Oh?"

"You don't get many requests like this, I take it."

"Actually, I've had two, both from men."

"Why not women, do you suppose?"

"I think it's because women can pass off a psychic gift as women's intuition. They're more comfortable with it."

"Did you have any success with those men?"

"The first one just talked to me one day and decided not to go through with any treatment. For the second I used hypnosis and never heard from him again, so I don't know if it was successful. There's still not much known about the phenomenon. Doing away with it isn't as easy as giving a shot of antibiotics to get rid of a viral infection. First of all, I'd have to establish what kind of psychic gifts you have—ESP, psychokinesis, precognition . . ."

"I have ESP and precognition. It's the precognition I have to get rid of."

"The ability to see into the future is a talent many people would envy. What bothers you about it?"

The turquoise eyes flashed with impatience. "Look, I don't want to waste time getting heavily into the psychodynamics of this thing. Name your fee and I'll pay it. Will you use hypnosis?"

The urgency of Dylan Hamlin's tone disturbed her. Something frightening must have happened to him recently. She'd have to know more before she could help him, and it would probably not be easy. Most men would not admit to fear, especially to a woman.

"I might use hypnosis if I thought it would help. But even then I wouldn't suggest you try to do away with it completely. I'd probably give you a post-hypnotic suggestion that you still have visions of future events, but they would occur only in dreams and you wouldn't remember them on waking."

"Why not just get rid of it?"

"It may not be wise. Those gifts may be there for a reason."

His expression darkened and he stood up. "Don't give me any metaphysical mumbo jumbo about my possessing 'special spiritual gifts.' I don't buy it."

"Sit down," she said gently. "Neither do I. I'm speaking strictly as a medical psychologist. It's only in recent years that we've discovered the importance of dreams. People deprived of them begin to develop psychotic symptoms. Precognition may fall into the same category. For all we know, everyone may have the ability to see into the future. Didn't you ever walk into a room and think you'd been there before, but knew it was impossible?"

"Many times."

"It's called *déjà vu,* and it's happened to everyone. Just now we're beginning to think the reasons behind it are that we're reliving a dream."

"You're just coming to that conclusion?"

"Do your premonitions usually occur in dreams?"

"Except at the racetrack."

Sonia was intrigued. "You can pick winners?" There had recently been some well-documented cases on the phenomenon.

"All that's irrelevant to what I need at the moment," he said abruptly. "Do you have time to do the hypnosis today? I've got an appointment over at the Burbank Studios at two-thirty."

"Are you an actor?"

"Stuntman."

"That's very dangerous work."

"It can be." He dismissed it with an indifferent shrug.

"Wouldn't the ability to foresee events come in handy in your line of work? I'd think being forewarned of a disastrous stunt could save your life."

"It has—several times, in fact."

"For example," she pressed.

He gazed at her with grudging amusement. "You don't give up easily, do you?"

"My training. And if I'm going to help you, I have to know more about you."

He sat back in the chair. "All right. I'll tell you about one incident. Did you see *Battle for Andromeda*?"

Sonia shook her head. "It could have been the last movie on earth and I probably wouldn't have seen it. I don't go to movies much."

"It was one of those outer-space adventure films. We were on location in the Mohave Desert for a battle scene. These space warriors in silvery costumes were getting laser-gunned off huge futuristic tanklike contraptions. I did my fall off the tank and I was supposed to lie there while they got a shot of it. But as I was lying on the sand, I suddenly had a vision of a heavy piece of metal coming loose and falling on me."

"What did you do?"

"Got up and walked away." He chuckled. "The director was madder than a hornet, screaming at me to get back there. I was ruining his shot. Two seconds later a big chunk of metal dropped off the tank. Had I still been lying there, it would have killed me."

"If your precognition has proved that useful, I don't understand why you would want to get rid of it."

"Because there are other times . . ." He looked out the window. When he turned back to her he spoke softly, the Southern intonations more pronounced than ever.

"There are other other times—like when you're about to take a fifty-foot fall off an office building into an air bag. You've rehearsed, calculated your trajectory—everything down to the split second. Then suddenly you see yourself splattered on the pavement. Stuntmen and women without any psychic ability have that sort of feeling all the time. It's called fear. And contrary to popular belief, good stunt people aren't daredevils; we're after a good illusion on film. Fear is damn healthy for a stuntman; it's what makes you double-check the air bag for leaks. What hangs me up is not knowing if I'm dealing with fear or precognition. And in this business you've got to be thinking with a clear mind, or you *will* find yourself splattered on the pavement."

That he had admitted his fear was a good start, but she needed more.

"What made you decide to go into stunt work for a living?"

"What made you go into psychology? I love it. I'm good at it. If you're hinting that I have some deep-seated need to self-destruct, you're on the wrong track."

Sonia didn't want to contradict him at this point in their relationship, but she suspected from the sudden belligerent tone that either he was lying about his motives or he didn't know them himself.

"I'm curious," she said. "You've obviously had this problem with stunts and premonitions for a while. Why the urgency to get rid of it now?"

"It never occurred to me that one could get rid of it. Then I read that article about your research in the *L.A. Times*. I thought maybe I'd give you a try."

"That article appeared three months ago, and you're just now coming to see me. I think you're evading the real reason. Something must have happened recently to make you more aware of your abilities."

A smile started at the edges of his mouth. "You're perceptive, Dr. Barnes."

"It's my job to be. What happened?"

"I have a stunt coming up that is going to take split-second timing. I can't afford to have my mind muddled up. It's for a spy thriller. According to the script, the villain has kidnapped the spy's girlfriend and he's got her in the back seat of an open convertible, driving down a deserted road. The spy is in a helicopter overhead. To rescue the girl, he's got to climb down a cable ladder and hang upside down from a trapeze bar attached to the end of it. Then the girl reaches up, he grabs her wrists and lifts her out of the car. The helicopter rises up to about a hundred fifty feet with the two of them hanging at the end of the ladder."

Sonia's mouth was dry. "I take it you're the one who'll be hanging upside down from the helicopter and rescuing the girl."

"The star of the movie sure as hell isn't going to do it."

It was hard to imagine anyone letting himself be put through an experience like that. He had to have a death wish. "And you've been having nightmares about this stunt."

"Almost every night. I dream that I'm being dropped down too low to the side of the car. I see the rear wheel spinning beside me; then my head hits the pavement."

He stood up and walked to the window. This was not a man content to sit quietly for any period of time. If he couldn't relax, he'd be difficult to hypnotize.

"Everyone has dreams about things that are bothering them," she said. "In this case I think it's quite understandable. Your dreaming about the accident doesn't necessarily mean it's going to happen. It could just be a way your mind has of dealing with the fear you're trying to suppress."

"Exactly why I need to be hypnotized."

"But if it's only a bad dream, there are other ways to deal with it. Perhaps if we discussed the dream in detail, your feelings about the stunt—"

"You don't believe I'm psychic, do you?" he interrupted her.

"Mr. Hamlin, in the course of my research I've run across many people who think they are psychic but who have no ability I can measure in a lab. That doesn't mean they do not have psychic ability, just that it doesn't show up in a controlled lab environment. Whether you are or aren't may not be pertinent to my being able to help you."

His eyes narrowed. "If you don't believe I'm psychic, you can't possibly help me."

"Not necessarily." She spoke quietly and was glad to see him take the chair again. "I had a patient once who was troubled by feelings of anxiety he couldn't put a finger on and suggested that through hypnosis I regress him to a past life. He saw himself as a medieval knight in a jousting tournament where he accidently killed a king of France. It was all very colorful and interesting and the event itself was well documented in history."

"Evidence of reincarnation?" Dylan asked.

"Utterly inconclusive. It might have been the remembered scene from a book or a movie. But the important thing was that after our session, he lost his feelings of anxiety and was able to continue on with his life. Scientific inquiry aside, helping people is the ultimate goal of any of this."

"Look, I am psychic and I can establish it for you very quickly. Give me your hands. No, palms up." He touched her fingertips and she felt a shock. Was it that electro-psychic energy that showed up as an aura on her Kirlian photographs? The longer their fingers touched, the more the delicious tingling spread through her body.

He closed his eyes, and for the first time he seemed to reach a state of relaxation. Perhaps hypnotizing him wouldn't be that difficult after all.

She studied the lean, rugged contours of his face, the aquiline nose and black eyebrows, the way his eyelashes cast shadows on his cheeks. His voice was good, and he had a commanding presence and photogenic features. He could have been an actor if he'd wanted to be in movies. Why would he choose to make a living hanging upside down from a trapeze bar at an altitude of a hundred and fifty feet?

Suddenly his eyelids fluttered in what was usually an indication of hypnotic trance. Sonia watched him with interest.

"A child, small child, kneeling beside something. It's a little boy, dark hair beside . . . water, a creek or a stream . . ." His voice trailed off then came back, the Southern accent more pronounced. "You're there and very young— about nine or ten it seems, ten, the number ten comes to me. You have long black braids tied with pink ribbons and you're wearing something pink, a dress with tiny rosebuds on the collar."

Sonia's cheeks flushed. She knew now what he was seeing. There was no way he could have known. She'd never told anyone in Los Angeles. Could he sense the tension racing through her fingertips? The memory of the scene was coming back to her now in vivid detail. The nightmare that never quite left her no matter how many years separated her from that awful day.

"The little boy has something in his hand . . . a glass jar?"

She hadn't meant to say anything but caught herself murmuring, "He was catching polly-wogs."

"Something moving up the hill . . . a kid a little bit older than you . . . blond . . . you're running to him."

Her hands were shaking so violently now that she dropped them from his. Part of her wished he would stop, but in spite of the unexpected emotional turmoil, she was intrigued.

Hands shaking, she gave him her fingertips again.

"The little boy by the river is . . ." Dylan's lips moved and there was a crease between his eyebrows. "The boy is facedown in the water."

Dylan opened his eyes. "He died, didn't he?"

Sonia nodded. "He slipped on a rock, hit his head."

"He was someone close to you. Who?"

"My little brother."

"And the other kid, also your brother?"

"No, he was a . . . friend, a boyfriend, actually."

Dylan studied her eyes. "I upset you. I'm sorry."

She smiled to reassure him. "It's all right. It was really quite an extraordinary demonstration of your psychic ability. I'm just surprised you picked up on something so remote in my past."

"Not so remote as all that," he said softly.

"I suppose not."

"Could you tell me what happened exactly?"

She didn't like to talk about it. In fact, it had been years since she had, and then only to a psychiatrist. But Dylan had seen it and he might as well know the details.

She spoke haltingly. "The dress you saw . . . my grandmother had given it to me for my tenth birthday. My brother and I were at her ranch in San Diego for Christmas vacation. There was a creek running through the back of the property. I'd just met the other boy. His name was Charlie. I knew he was coming over and I wanted to show off my new dress. That day I was supposed to watch my little brother and I resented it. When I saw Charlie I guess I rebelled. I ran up the hill to see him, and when I came back, Jay Jay was . . . lying there . . ."

She gathered herself together and did her best to resume a professional tone. "Psychics generally pick up on events of a strong emotional impact."

"That's usually what I get—if I pick up at all. With some people there's nothing, but I felt an immediate communication with you—even back in the hospital parking lot."

"You saw me in the parking lot?" she asked with surprise.

"Mentally cataloging my surroundings is an old habit that comes in handy in my work. Not much gets by me, certainly not such an attractive woman."

She thought it best not to acknowledge the compliment. "Interesting that you'd see a detail like the rosebuds on the collar of my dress."

"They must have meant something to you."

"They were why I loved the dress. Can you see just as clearly into the future?"

"I see scenes of a life like on a film reel unwinding. If I can roll the film backward, I can usually roll it forward."

"Try it on me," she said lightly.

He held out his hands. She wondered if the touch would again make her tingle and found herself anxiously hoping it would. The shock wasn't there this time, but the slow tingle once again traveled up her arms and spread lazily through her. It might be some electro-psychic energy, but anyone who didn't know from such things would probably have called the sensation erotic.

He closed his eyes, and once again she saw his eyelids flutter. "A young man with a narrow mouth, kind of frizzy blond hair . . . I get bad feelings about him—as though he were trying to harm you in some way."

Walt Anguin? Her lab assistant fitted the description, but he was the last person in the world

who would do her any harm. "Do you see anything else?"

Dylan dropped his hands from hers, opened
his eyes and began to smile.

"What is it?"

The smile broke into a grin, and she was taken
by how ruggedly attractive he was with the
smile lines creasing the sides of his mouth and
corners of his eyes, the white teeth contrasting
with his tan.

"I'm not sure you want to know what I saw."

"Was it funny?"

"No."

"Then why are you smiling?"

He took a deep breath and let it out slowly, his
eyes sparkling. "You really want to know?"

"What did you see?"

He began reluctantly. "A colorful room, reds
and blues and yellows and big modern graphic
paintings, a red bedspread."

"My bedroom," she said with delight.

"White furniture—sleek, modern . . . bright
blue carpet."

His grin broadened.

"Is that all?"

"No. On the bed . . . Look, I don't want to
embarrass you."

Did he think she'd be embarrassed by the
giant Raggedy Ann doll? It would be an extraordinary detail. "Go on. I hear all sorts of things in
my work. Not much shocks me."

"This might."

"What is it?"

He sat back in the chair, this time without the

smile, but his eyes remained intense under the thick black lashes.

Even before he spoke she felt a tremor in her depths, almost as if she knew what he was going to say before he said it.

"On the bed I saw you and me . . . making love."

Chapter 2

"I DON'T DOUBT YOUR SINCERITY," SHE SAID with a professional calm she didn't feel. "You obviously picked up on the decor of my bedroom, but the rest . . ."

"You think it was just wishful thinking on my part?"

She had to suppress a smile. "It certainly was not evidence of precognition."

"Unless you and I do end up making love."

"Of course," she was forced to admit. "But it is very unlikely, if I'm going to be seeing you on a professional basis, that we would develop that kind of a relationship."

"Perhaps I do have a vivid imagination."

Or I do, she thought wryly. It was hard to look at Dylan Hamlin without being beset by dangerously erotic thoughts. There was every possibility he was picking up her desires, not his. The scientist in her briefly wondered about the phenomenon. Was there strong ESP between people who were attracted to each other?

Sonia had to remind herself that this was no cocktail party game where such an attraction could result in a personal relationship. To become involved would break every code of professional ethics.

"When can we do the hypnosis?"

"I have to be in my lab in a few minutes, but if you'd like to make an appointment for another day, I'll be glad to give it a try."

They agreed on a time the following week and he stood up to leave. As he reached the door he turned. "What sort of lab work are you doing?"

"You're welcome to come along and observe. I'm conducting an experiment today in extrasensory perception."

He checked his watch. "Why not? Are you trying to prove ESP exists?"

"That's already been proven. I'm experimenting with ways to make it occur in a laboratory environment, which doesn't seem to be the most conducive atmosphere for it."

"I wouldn't think so."

"Most early ESP experiments were done with cards," she explained. "A person sat in one room and looked at a card with a geometric shape on it while another tried to visualize either the circle, square or triangle."

"Sounds boring."

"That may have been the reason why the

scores were so low. Most instances of ESP seem to occur when the sender is in a highly charged emotional state. I read a case where a child was hit by a car, and his mother, a hundred miles away, cried out in pain."

"So the trick is to get people emotionally charged up. How do you manage that without putting them in mortal danger?"

"I'll show you."

They walked down the hall to the laboratory, where her assistant was setting up the equipment. She considered herself fortunate in having found Walt Anguin. A graduate student in psychology, he was enthusiastic about psychical research and a whiz with mechanical devices. However, with his frizzy blond hair and thin lips, he was disturbingly close in appearance to the man Dylan had described.

Remembering what Dylan had said, Sonia felt embarrassed, then guilty, as though she were withholding an important secret from Walt. But what could she tell him? Hey, Walt, this guy thinks you're out to do me in. Of course, he's never met you before in his life, but . . . It was as preposterous as her making love one day to Dylan Hamlin in her bedroom.

Dylan walked around the lab inspecting the equipment. "This is an isolation booth, isn't it? What do you use it for?"

"We don't want the subject to have any outside stimuli so we can be sure that what he is receiving is ESP and not sound waves."

"And the video tape recorder?"

"The person in the isolation booth watches a

videotape while his partner in another room tries to pick up on what he's seeing."

Dylan examined one of the videocassettes, marked "War." "What's on the tapes?"

"Scenes that should have a strong emotional impact on the viewer."

He nodded in approval. "Clever. Does it work?"

Before she could continue, they were interrupted by the appearance of two exuberant teenagers, sisters who claimed to have had numerous psychic experiences. Sonia had been glad to find them. An accumulation of case histories seemed to support the theory that people closely related had more instances of ESP.

"Ah, you're here, good," she said. "Let's get started. Walt, are the tapes ready?"

"Everything is," he answered crisply. Sonia didn't have to ask. Whatever she asked Walt to do was always taken care of efficiently.

The older sister pointed at Dylan and whispered to Sonia, "Is he part of the experiment?"

"No," said Sonia with amusement, "he's just observing."

Both girls looked crestfallen. What a shame she couldn't put him in the isolation booth with one of the sisters, Sonia thought wryly. He elicited exactly the kind of strong emotional response she was looking for.

"Who wants to be the transmitter and who wants to be the receiver?" Walt asked them.

"Who does what?" asked the older girl.

"The transmitter sits in the isolation booth and watches the tapes, and the receiver lies down in the other room and tries to pick them up through ESP."

"I'll be the receiver," the younger one piped up.

"That's because you're so lazy," her sister chided sarcastically. "All you do is lie around all day."

Sonia showed the girl to the adjacent room and told her to get comfortable on the bed.

"Your sister is going to be watching videotapes that we hope will have a strong emotional impact on her. They will last for exactly one minute. Your job is to receive these impressions. Any feelings, thoughts, images, any sort of free associations, please speak them into the microphone."

"What if I don't get any impression at all?"

"Then say so."

Though staying in the background, Dylan watched all these preliminaries with fascination.

The first videotape, "War," was straight off the evening news, a full minute of disturbing battle scenes complete with sound effects.

The girl in the other room was saying into the microphone, "I'm not seeing anything, maybe like an ocean, waves or something . . ."

Sonia shook her head and signaled for Walt to put in the next tape. It was a lively Fred Astaire tap dance number.

The girl lying down said, "I'm thinking of our cat. I can't remember if I fed him this morning."

Dylan gave her a thumbs-down.

At the end of the session after five tapes, there

were no correlations. The girls were disappointed.

"I got such a definite impression of Fred on that second tape," said the younger sister.

"Fred?" asked Sonia with surprise. "You said you saw your cat."

"Yeah. Our cat Fred. He's black and white and looks like he's wearing a tuxedo, so my dad named him Fred Astaire."

"You idiot," said her sister. "The videotape was a Fred Astaire dance routine."

"That should count, then." Walt turned to the older girl. "Did you think about your cat Fred during the dance routine?"

"I don't remember, exactly, but I might have. When we were little we used to lift Fred up and make him dance around." She giggled. "We even got him a little top hat."

The minute they left, Dylan turned to her. "I want to try it."

She was thrilled that it had sparked his interest. "Do you have a partner you want to bring in, or would you like me to set you up with someone?"

"No, I want to do it right now. With you in the isolation booth and me receiving."

"That's impossible. I'm running the experiment. I can't be in it. It wouldn't be a fair test. I already know all the tapes."

"What difference would that make as long as I'm the one receiving? Do you have any tapes other than the ones we just saw?"

"I have another set, but . . ."

"Then use them. You'll be watching tapes I haven't seen before."

"I'll do it with you," Walt offered.

"You know all the tapes too," Sonia reminded him.

Dylan shook his head. "I want Dr. Barnes as a partner. I already know I can pick up impressions from her."

"You do?" Walt looked at them with surprise. "How?"

"A little experiment we did back in the office," said Sonia. "Mr. Hamlin appears to be a talented psychic."

"I think you ought to try it, then," said Walt enthusiastically. "We don't have to make the results official or anything."

She shrugged. "Okay, why not?"

The small bed was almost too short for Dylan's long frame. Sonia watched him stretch out and put himself easily into a state of deep relaxation. She hoped he wasn't picking up anything from her just then, because the sight of him like that sent her senses into overload.

"He in the movies or something?" Walt asked as she stepped into the isolation booth.

"Stuntman," said Sonia.

"Oh. One of those."

"One of what?"

"A loony. From what I've heard, they're all loonies."

"Don't you think that's a rather unfair generalization?"

Walt wrinkled his upper lip. "No."

Sonia tried to put Dylan out of her mind and concentrate on the first tape. It was a tranquil forest scene with sunbeams streaming through pine needles. There was a peaceful chatter of birds, the scurrying of little animals. She had chosen it because it gave her a strong sense of contentment and well-being.

Unable to keep her attention focused, however, she found her mind wandering back to Dylan Hamlin.

She halted that train of thought. What if Dylan picked it up and spoke it into the microphone? She'd die of embarrassment if Walt heard.

The next tape was of a roller coaster ride. Her father had taken her on one as a child and she'd screamed in terror at the top of her lungs the whole way. Grasping the armrests of the chair in the isolation booth, she held her breath and wondered if Dylan would pick up on her remembered fear.

She was glad the next video was a happy one: circus clowns cavorting and calliope music. She even laughed out loud at the antics. The next tape was of a thundering herd of wild horses stampeding, and the final tape showed an electric modern dance sequence.

She joined Dylan in the lab, anxious to see the result.

Looking more pale than usual, Walt brushed a frizzy lock from his forehead. "This is a new one on me."

"How'd I do?" Dylan asked.

Walt shook his head. "You missed every one."

Dylan's face dropped. "You're kidding! But I was picking up some very definite images, especially at the beginning."

Walt looked helplessly at Sonia. "I just don't know how to interpret something like this."

"What do you mean?"

"Here, look at the chart. I jotted down his comments alongside each tape. I've never seen anything like this before."

As Sonia looked over the chart, her mouth fell open. She suddenly understood what had Walt so frazzled. Out of the five tapes, only the first three were significant, but those made her heart race. It was the breakthrough she had been hoping for.

TRANSMITTER'S VIDEOTAPE	RECEIVER'S COMMENTS
1. Forest scene	"My chest feels tight, like fear . . . zooming up and down . . . riding in little cars . . . swerving around corners."
2. Roller coaster	"Lots of movement, people in colorful costumes like clowns in a circus . . . jumping up and down."

3. Clowns

"I'm not picking up much at all, maybe the color blue like sky, flying."

Sonia clapped her hands together excitedly. "This is extraordinary! For the first two you described what was going to be on the *next* tape in the series.

He looked disappointed. "Only those two?"

"Only!" Walt slapped the side of his head. "That's two out of five, way above chance. You were *predicting*, man. That was precognition. We've never had that happen before. Sometimes somebody will pick a tape that's just been run, but never the very next one."

"That's what I was hoping for."

"You were *trying* to do that?" Walt asked with amazement.

"Dr. Barnes was skeptical about my having precognition. I wanted to prove I did."

Walt swallowed and turned to Sonia. "He was *trying* to do that, for God's sake. Trying! That means he can control it. Hey man, you've got to come back and do some more experiments."

"Wait a minute," Sonia said carefully. "What you did is not necessarily evidence of precognition."

"It has to be," argued Walt. "What else could it be?"

"He could have been getting ESP from you."

"But he was picking the next tape in the series."

"But Walt, you knew what the next one would be, didn't you?"

He pulled thoughtfully at a frizzy tuft of blond hair. "That's true. I laid all the cassettes out ahead of time. We'll have to change the experiment so that nobody knows what tape is coming up."

"That's easy enough," said Dylan. "Next time just don't label them, and arrange them in a random sequence."

"Would you be willing to come back for another experiment?" asked Sonia.

"Sure," he said quickly.

"If we're going to try and measure your ability to see into the future, it would mean postponing the hypnosis," she reminded him. "Are you sure you want to put it off?"

"No problem," he said easily. "The helicopter stunt isn't until next month. Most of my life I've been telling people I could do this, and nobody believed me even when things turned out like I said. So this would be like having one last chance to prove I was right."

"I still think it's best we don't use me as your partner," said Sonia. "Is there anyone with whom you've had some ESP?"

"A stuntwoman I know. I'm sure she'd be happy to do it if she's not working that day."

"Have you ever done predicting with any consistency before?" asked Walt.

"Just at the horse races."

Walt's eyes lit up. "You can pick winners?"

"Fairly often."

Walt whistled through his teeth. "There was a study on that recently, wasn't there, Dr. Barnes?"

"A couple of them. My favorite was about the elderly lady who closed her eyes and let her pencil drop on the racing form the night before. When she was tested, she picked the right horse about a third of the time over a six-week period. That alone was pretty astounding statistically."

Walt had a greedy look in his eye as he dug around in his briefcase. "I've got my racing form right here. Can you pick them like that?"

Dylan laughed. "Unfortunately, that doesn't work for me. I've found I have to be at the track, watching the horses in the parade ring. Listen, I was going out there tomorrow afternoon. Why don't you all come along and I'll give you a demonstration?"

Walt was practically salivating at the thought. "We ought to do it, Dr. Barnes."

"Sure, Walt. How am I going to explain spending the afternoon at the racetrack to Dr. McCabe?"

"We'll set it up as a legitimate experiment," said Walt. "I'll be the control."

"What's a control?" asked Dylan.

"Scientists have all these dumb little rules," he explained. "Like when they test out a new drug, they give placebos to a control group to see if they show any improvement. And the key word in an experiment is *repeatable*. Nobody believes your results unless everyone in the world can repeat what you've done at least a hundred times. The rules wreak havoc with things like ESP because by its very nature it's unpredictable."

"How are you going to use controls in a race-track experiment?"

"I'll be one control by choosing horses according to regular handicapping methods. Dr. Barnes can be another control by betting hunches. And you'll use your precognition. We'll see who does the best."

"It's an intriguing idea," she admitted. "I don't suppose one afternoon would hurt, but we'd really need to go a lot more times to give us any significant statistics. They had six weeks of statistics with that other horse-racing experiment, and there is no way we could spare that amount of time to go to the track. So I can't see getting started."

"Aren't you curious?" Walt persisted. "Even if we just went once, it would be a way of testing Dylan to see if what happened in the lab today was just a fluke."

She sighed. "Oh, all right."

"Good, then it's settled," said Dylan. "I'll pick you all up here tomorrow at noon and treat you to lunch at the Turf Club."

He held out his hand. "It's been a pleasure, Walt, Dr. Barnes."

Sonia shook his hand and was surprised to feel the tingling spread through her again. This time something in Dylan's eyes told her he felt it too.

Did the Pentagon know how naked you felt when somebody could read your thoughts?

Chapter 3

WALT AND SONIA MET DYLAN IN THE HOSPITAL parking lot at noon the following day.

"Figures a stuntman would have a car like that," Walt muttered under his breath as Dylan pulled into a parking space.

"It looks nice. What kind of a car is it?" She knew as much about cars as she did about movies.

"A '67 Cobra Shelby 500. About the most expensive Mustang you can get, a collector's item, real high-performance stock car. I'm surprised he left it plain black. I'd figure a stuntman would paint big gold stripes down the side."

Before she could comment on his sarcasm, Dylan was out of the car and coming toward them. Sonia was aware of her heart pumping at a quicker pace. He was wearing tan Levis and a blue polo shirt that set off the turquoise eyes and did nothing to hide the hard, well-honed muscles of his torso.

He gave her an admiring look. "Good to see you."

She suddenly wished she'd worn something a bit flashier than a drab beige "professor" pantsuit. She'd dressed for work, not the races, though she'd made an exception to her usual rule and wore a brighter shade of lipstick and some eyeliner.

Walt climbed into the back seat while Sonia took the front one. She might not know much about cars, but this one definitely seemed to fit Dylan Hamlin. If it had been a black stallion, it would have been chomping at the bit to run.

"You go to the racetrack often?" she asked Dylan as they turned onto the Ventura Freeway.

"Often as I can. I love the horses."

"To ride them or just to bet on them?" Walt asked.

"I do some stunt riding now and then, but unfortunately, hardly anyone's making Westerns anymore. I used to do equestrian acrobatics in the circus."

"You were a circus performer?" She found it amusing and slightly titillating to imagine him in one of those tight-fitting sequined costumes, leaping about on the backs of galloping white horses.

"For six years."

"Were you from a family of performers?"

"No. When I was thirteen I ran away from home to join the circus."

"You're kidding," said Walt. "I thought that just happened in legends."

"It happens more often than anyone would care to believe."

"Why did you run away from home?" asked Walt.

"It's a long story."

Sonia immediately sensed it was a story she would have to know if she was going to get at the cause of his recurring nightmare.

Dylan turned to her. "You ever played the horses?"

"I've never even been to a racetrack before."

"Horse racing falls under Dr. Barnes's category of mindless pastimes," said Walt.

Dylan's dark eyebrows rose. "What have you got against mindless pastimes?"

Walt answered for her with an edge of sarcasm. "She prides herself on a strict avoidance of passive activities. That means television and movies, even listening to records."

"You don't like music?" Dylan asked with surprise.

"Love it. I play the piano for a couple of hours every day, and I like to sing. I've even written songs. I'd just rather do it than listen to it."

He shot her a look of admiration. "I like your attitude. It's my private theory that there's a national conspiracy afloat to brainwash people into becoming docile, passive consumers of entertainment. Look at the current video game craze, kids who should be out playing baseball on a sunny day burying themselves in neon arcades."

"At least they're out making social contact," said Sonia, "and not stuck at home alone vegetating in front of a TV set."

"If everybody had your aversion to television, Dylan would be out of business," observed Walt.

"You're absolutely right. I should be grateful for passive, mindless audiences. They keep me off the unemployment line. You don't read books either?"

"That's in a different category. With books you can do some active imagining. But I'd rather write and create my own fantasies."

He gave her an oblique look as he shifted gears. "You must have an active imagination."

"Very."

"I suspected as much," he said slyly. "So do I."

"I believe we already established that."

He grinned at her. "That was precognition."

"What was?" asked Walt.

Sonia blushed and continued to face front so that he couldn't see it from the back seat. "Oh, nothing."

"I made a little prediction about Dr. Barnes that she would rather attribute to my vivid imagination than any psychic ability."

Sonia suddenly remembered his prediction about Walt and quickly dismissed it again.

"I've always felt you could divide the entire world population into the actives and the passives," said Dylan.

"You're an active, I suppose," said Sonia.

"Definitely. I'd much rather be doing stunt work than sitting in a movie house watching someone else do it on the screen."

"Then why would you bother with a spectator sport like horse racing?" noted Walt.

"Hell, that's not passive. Not if you're betting."

Suddenly Dylan swerved around a car to make a lane change, then switched back again, wedging tightly between two cars.

"All right," said Sonia, clutching the seat. "We're impressed with your stunt-driving ability, so you can go back to driving normally now."

"Sorry. Didn't mean to scare you. You're not much on roller coasters either, I gathered from yesterday."

"That kind of fear would probably be hard for you to grasp."

"Not really," he said thoughtfully. "Roller coasters are a thrill a minute, but they're also passive vehicles. You just sit there while it gives you a ride. I'd rather be in a car where I have some control. It's like my buddy Quinn, who's a stunt pilot. He's scared to death to fly in commercial planes though he'll do the wildest things in a helicopter or a single-engine. As long as he's in control, he's fine."

Walt was studying a racing form in the back seat. "Have you checked out any of the horses in today's race?"

"I never look at that stuff. When I see the right horse, I know."

"You win a lot of money?"

"On good days."

"You mean you aren't consistent?" She had let herself be conned into this experiment by

Dylan, who wanted to prove his precognition, and by Walt, who was after a fast buck. And although she was enjoying the afternoon off, it could prove to be a waste of time.

"Some days are better than others," said Dylan. "When I first came out to California and wasn't working as much and needed money, I spent a lot of time at the track, and more often than not I came home with the rent money and a little over. I've got a feeling I'm going to go home richer today."

"I hope I don't disappoint you," said Sonia, "but I've given this some thought and decided we shouldn't actually bet any money on the races."

"What?" He looked at her as though she should be fitted for a straitjacket. "What's the fun if you don't place a bet or two?"

"Yeah," Walt chimed in. "You can't go to the track and not place a bet. It's sacrilegious."

"But we're doing this experiment under the auspices of the University of Los Angeles. They are going to take a dim view of our spending the day at the track anyway, so why make it worse by spending the university's money on pari-mutuel tickets?"

"I never was expecting to use the university's money," said Dylan. "In fact, I insist on using my own. I'm not sure my psychic ability would even shift into gear if I didn't have something at stake. Remember what you said about strong emotions being necessary?"

"That's an excellent point," said Walt.

"How about if we pretend to place two-dollar bets," she suggested. "Wouldn't that be just as good?"

"Two dollars each race," he said flatly. "How can you get riled up over a mere two dollars— and an imagined two dollars, at that."

"I thought you had a good imagination," Sonia teased.

"Not that good."

"How about a compromise?" she said. "We let Dylan place bets but Walt and I simply pretend to."

"That throws the experiment off kilter," complained Walt. "If one does it, then we all have to do it."

"All right, then, but we should all be limited to two-dollar bets. How many races are there?"

"Nine," said Walt. "That only comes to eighteen dollars each. I can't see where anybody at ULA could complain about that. Most of the people in our department go through more than that in rat pellets."

She reluctantly agreed. "But any winnings you and I make, Walt, we put back into our budget."

"Wait a minute," he whined indignantly. "What we win, we should keep! In fact, I don't see where we even owe them the eighteen dollars apiece. This is a legitimate experiment expense."

She sighed. "Okay, okay. You do whatever you want with your winnings if you have any, but I'm putting mine back into the department. I have enough trouble with McCabe over expenses like film for our Kirlian camera."

Dylan Hamlin was obviously a regular at San Felipe Meadows. The maître d' at the Turf Club greeted him like an old friend and gave them an excellent table for lunch. Despite Sonia's protests, Dylan insisted on treating them all.

Gambling at the races fitted in with what she already knew about his personality. A former circus acrobat and stuntman would have to be willing to take risks in life. It even reflected in the way he drove a car.

She was completely the opposite, a cautious driver who always let the other guy go first and waited until she had plenty of room to make a lane change. On a trip to Las Vegas a few years before, she'd even been reluctant to risk anything more than a few dollars on slot machines.

"You've never had any dreams of winners at the track?" asked Sonia as she started her seafood salad.

"Not that I remember. And it's odd, now that I think of it. Usually when I have premonitions, they come to me in dreams."

"In all the material we could find on the subject, people always dreamed their winners," said Walt. "One lady saw the horse in her dream cross the finish line and heard the announcer give the name. This happened night after night until finally her husband started checking out the tracks all over the country. Inevitably those horses were running and they'd won."

"The couple must have cleaned up," said Dylan.

"They were very religious and didn't believe in gambling," said Walt. "But then they talked to their minister and he suggested the dreams might be a gift from God. So they started betting and won enough to buy themselves a camper they'd been wanting for a long time. And then a strange thing happened—the dreams stopped."

"I'll have to start concentrating," Dylan mused. "Maybe I am dreaming winners. It would be a lot easier to use a bookie than drive all the way to San Felipe, though I love it out here, the excitement, the color . . ."

"Maybe that's why you don't remember the dream," Sonia suggested. "Your subconscious won't allow it because, if you did, you'd have to forgo the pleasure of coming out here."

He considered it. "You're probably right. When I see a horse in the parade ring, sometimes that feeling comes over me—like you were talking about yesterday, the *déjà vu*. This is fascinating. Tell me about the other cases."

"There was another woman who claimed she saw the winning number on a horse as he crossed the finish line."

"A useless dream," added Walt. "The number did her no good because she didn't know the name of the horse or where it was running."

"It must have driven her crazy."

"It was driving her husband crazy," said Sonia. "Then one day she woke up with a feeling that if they bet a certain number on the local daily double, they'd win $500. He hauled her out to the track that day and, against his better judgment, bet the horse even though it was an incredible long shot. They won $497 and then her dreams never occurred again."

Dylan took a long sip of his beer. "I guess I should be thankful. I may have good days and bad ones, but at least the ability to predict doesn't ever go entirely."

"After I hypnotize you that may happen," Sonia cautioned.

A grave look of concern crossed his face. "How about a posthypnotic suggestion that it would still work at the track?"

"I could try, but there'd be no guarantee on that either."

He finished his beer and glanced back up at the stands. "There are forty thousand people out here today who don't know if they're going to win or lose, and they're still having a good time. There's no reason why I can't come to the track for the fun of it too. In fact, the suspense could make it just that much more exciting."

"Don't delude yourself. The fun of it is winning," said Walt.

Dylan's comment put the stunt nightmare into perspective for Sonia. He enjoyed horse races a great deal, but he was willing to forgo a constant winning streak to rid himself of the pain that dream seemed to be causing.

"Tell Dylan about the other case, the film producer," Walt suggested.

"Who was it? Maybe I've worked for him."

"The article I read didn't give his name," said

Sonia. "But it was well documented. He had a vivid dream where he saw two horses neck and neck and heard the announcer call out the winner. Friends finally convinced him to check it out, and he learned that the horse was running the following week. He went out to the track with the eeriest feelings, especially when the two horses ended up neck and neck. It came down to a photo finish, and sure enough, his horse won."

"Did he have any more dreams?"

"Never again."

"That settles it," said Dylan with mock seriousness. "The dreams are rigged by the Racing Association. They tantalize you, then pull the rug out. It's all a scam to get you hooked on horse racing."

Near post time, they all went down to the walking ring so that Dylan could pick a horse for the first race.

The sight of the beautiful long-legged animals took Sonia's breath away. She loved watching the owners in their elegant clothes, the jockeys in their colorful silks. Dylan narrowed his eyes and walked slowly around the ring, focusing on first one horse, then the other. Finally he turned away and said, "Number nine."

Walt looked down at his racing form. "That's Flamenco Nights. Odds are ten to one. I'm going with the favorite, Wild Walter."

"You just picked that one because of the name!" said Sonia.

"Strictly scientific handicapping," he assured

her. "You're the one playing hunches. Which horse are you putting your money on?"

"I'm playing strictly feminist. I'm going with the woman jockey, number four."

"That's Sabina Carrasco," said Dylan. "Tough jockey. She's brought in quite a few winners for me."

Sonia looked over her program. "Hey, there are two jockeys named Carrasco in this race. Who's this M. Carrasco?"

"Her husband," said Dylan. "They both ride at San Felipe."

"I can imagine the things they yell at each other when they're coming down the stretch," said Sonia with a laugh. "Talk about a competitive marriage."

When they returned to the clubhouse to place their bets, Dylan was still grumbling good-naturedly about being limited to two dollars. It was a beautiful, sunny day, the sky a bright cerulean blue, unusual for Southern California. Desert winds had blown away any traces of smog, leaving the air fresh and clear. Palm trees were rustling, and horses, excited by the electricity in the air, were tossing their manes and prancing with mischief as they were led to the post.

Sonia grew tense as the thoroughbreds sprang out of the starting gate. Maybe Dylan was right. You had to have a bet in the race to make it exciting. As the horses flew down the stretch, Wild Walter was in the lead. Her horse was in fifth position and Dylan's was running third.

Then Dylan's horse, Flamenco Nights, began to move up.

"Come on, Flamenco!" Dylan jumped out of his chair to cheer him on, and soon Sonia and Walt were with him. Everyone around them was shouting as the horses scrambled to the finish line. It briefly occurred to Sonia as she was jumping up and down that this might not be the most scientific way to run an experiment, but it was certainly the most fun she'd ever had.

Flamenco Nights crossed the finish line first, winning by a length. Dylan let out a whoop, grabbed Sonia in a hug, lifted her high in the air and kissed her firmly on the lips. It all happened so quickly that she didn't have time to stop him, and during those few seconds the most wonderful sensations shot down to her toes. She was reluctant to let go of him.

As he put her down, he seemed suddenly to become aware of the brashness of his actions. "Sorry about that. I got carried away."

As Sonia tucked her blouse back in with trembling hands, she noticed Walt glaring darkly at her. "How'd your horse do, Walt?" she asked pleasantly, trying to make it seem as though nothing had happened.

"Placed fifth," he muttered.

Sonia looked at the toté board. "Hey, my woman jockey was third!"

"But you only bet to win, not to place," Walt informed her. "You won't get any money for it."

"Oh. Still, I think it's great she placed."

"Well, since I'm the only one in the money, I'm

buying us a round of drinks," Dylan announced, and went up to the window to cash in his ticket.

"He doesn't have to lord it over us," Walt muttered acidly as Dylan walked away.

"Walt, don't get so upset. This is just an experiment."

"And he had no business manhandling you in the process. Who does he think he is?"

"He just got carried away by the win."

"On a lousy two-dollar bet? That was just an excuse. The guy is trying to make it with you. And it doesn't look like you're trying to resist it, either."

In the two years she'd worked with Walt, this was the first time she could remember him ever directing a caustic comment of such a personal nature at her.

She felt obliged to smooth it over. "I think he was just a bit overexuberant. He's a very physical person. Look what he does for a living."

"Yeah, stunt work."

"What in the world do you have against stunt work?"

"Bunch of phonies in it who think they're hotshots and lady-killers."

"Have you known a lot of stuntpeople?"

"Well no, but I remember Burt Reynolds in that movie—"

"You're basing your prejudice on a movie? Talk about the brainwashed masses! Dylan Hamlin happens to be a very nice person and an extremely talented psychic. We're lucky he's cooperating with us on these experiments. In any case, a little hug is nothing to get worked up about."

But it was. Those few seconds in Dylan Hamlin's arms had been all too pleasant. Her knees still felt weak, and no matter how he touched her, even if it was just to hand her a drink, the electric tingling sensations still spread through her. There were even moments he looked at her, those turquoise eyes sparkling, that she felt her insides turn to molten lava. And whatever he did, from sipping a beer to shifting a gear, she found herself intrigued by his every movement. There had been men in Sonia's life who had attracted her before, but never with such magnetism.

What worried her was that if her reaction was obvious enough for Walt to notice, how would it appear to Dylan, who was already extremely sensitive to her? Under normal circumstances, she would simply accept it as the first stage in a potentially exciting romance. But if she was to deal successfully with his nightmares, she couldn't allow herself to become emotionally involved with him.

"Think you've got a winner in the next race?" Sonia asked Walt pleasantly to smooth over the tension.

Walt was sullenly bent over his racing form, making calculations with his pencil in the margins. "It's between two horses. They're both five-to-one shots and I can't decide."

Outside of their working relationship, Sonia had never given Walt much thought. He was one of those dependable fixtures in her life, always

on time, competent, efficient, a creative problem
solver. Did he have a lot of friends? Did he date
anyone steadily? The few times he'd been over
for dinner, it had always been with another
graduate student or faculty member to discuss
various research projects.

Now she was aware that, for some strange
reason, Walt had developed an intense dislike for
Dylan and it seemed to be coming to a head
today. With all the pressures of her job, the last
thing she needed was a personality conflict. As
she watched Walt leaning over his racing form,
running nervous fingers through his hair, Dylan's premonition didn't seem so farfetched. She
would have to be careful to stay sensitive to
Walt's feelings of hostility and avoid making it
worse. Unfortunately, there were such things as
self-fulfilling prophesies.

They watched the horses for the next race in
the walking ring.

"Number five," Dylan said finally.

Walt checked it on the program. "A twenty-to-
one shot named Ruffec, a French-bred horse
that did well in Europe but hasn't shown much
here yet. What's your horse?" he asked Sonia.

"I'm going with my lucky number, twelve."

"Good choice," said Walt. "That's one of the
favorites, Midnight Fury."

"Why is it your lucky number?" asked Dylan.

"My birthday is on December twelfth—twelfth
month, twelfth day."

"Good things happen to you with the number
twelve?"

She laughed. "Come to think of it, I don't

know. It's just always seemed a good number, kind of coincidental. But I guess it's because I associate it with all the fun and excitement of birthday parties. It's funny how people have their own little superstitions, more than just walking under ladders and avoiding black cats."

"I've never liked Tuesdays," said Dylan.

"Why?"

"I don't know. Maybe something bad happened to me on a Tuesday."

"I've never liked the number eight," said Walt. "And I can't think of any reason why that should be either, but I remember as a kid not wanting to be eight or, later, eighteen. And even though I consider myself a rational person, I'd never bet the eighth horse in the eighth race."

"Not even if that was the best choice?" asked Sonia.

Walt scratched his head with the eraser end of his pencil. "It is stupid, isn't it? I wonder what that horse has done." He buried himself back in the racing form and paid little attention when the horses sprang out of the starting gate again.

Dylan, uninhibited as ever, was yelling for his horse to come in, pummeling the railing with a rolled-up racing form.

"I think the reason you win is that the horse hears you and speeds up," Sonia laughed.

"Yeah? You could be right." He yelled even louder as the horses thundered down the stretch.

His French horse, however, either hadn't understood Dylan's English or had sent out a misleading translation in the walking ring. As the horses came up to the wire, Ruffec stumbled in second to last.

This time Walt's meticulous handicapping method paid off. His horse won.

"Why aren't you more excited?" asked Sonia.

Walt crumpled up a ticket angrily. "I put twenty dollars on our talented psychic's choice as well as the university's two dollars on mine." He glared at Dylan. "What the hell happened to your system?"

Dylan shrugged philosophically. "A wise circus fortune-teller once warned me that a soothsayer's predictions are never foolproof. Let that be a lesson to you."

In the third race none of their horses came close to finishing in the money. Sonia began to think that the day would be a washout as far as providing any statistics on precognition.

Then in the fourth race Dylan picked another winner, a forty-to-one shot. The big win put him in superb spirits. By the end of the day he had won three out of the nine races.

Walt had managed to pick one winner and two horses that placed. Sonia, playing whims and lucky numbers, had managed only one horse that placed, and no wins.

"Not much of a day for me," said Dylan as they walked out to the parking lot.

"You had an incredible day," Sonia protested.

"With only three out of nine races?"

"That's way above chance. It's very significant. I just wish we could do this more so I could build up statistics."

"I'm willing to continue." He gave her a devilish wink. "For the sake of science, of course."

Walt chuckled. "Can you imagine explaining our going to the horse races every afternoon to old Rat McCabe?"

"Who's Rat McCabe?"

"Dr. McCabe's the head of our department," Sonia explained. "We joke around that if an experiment doesn't involve rats, he thinks it's worthless. Needless to say, he doesn't care much for psychical research. This kind of experiment would drive him right up the wall."

"I have to admit it would drive me crazy to come out here and be limited to two-dollar bets."

"Do you really think you'd do better if you were risking more money?" she asked.

"Sure. There'd be more at stake. It's like you were saying about the importance of an emotional involvement. My premonitions are always the strongest when I'm in some kind of danger, and there's a degree of danger in losing money."

"It's something to consider," said Sonia. "We've never thought much about motivation in our ESP experiments. I wonder if our results would change if we devised some sort of reward for correct answers."

"Like what?" asked Walt.

"I don't know, maybe candy, a ticket to a movie. Dylan, what would motivate you— besides money?"

He unlocked the car door and gazed down at her. "You can't guess?" he said softly so that only she could hear.

She took a deep breath to steady herself. "Off limits," she murmured, and climbed into the back seat. "Walt," she called out cheerfully. "You can have the front seat on the way home."

"That should give you some indication about what she thinks of your driving," said Walt as he buckled his seatbelt.

The deliberate sneer in his voice raised the hackles on her neck. Suddenly she understood what was behind Walt's behavior. It was so basic, she wondered why she hadn't seen it before.

He was jealous.

Chapter 4

SONIA KNEW IT WAS UNWISE TO TAMPER WITH the staid, professorial image she'd worked so hard to create, but that morning something impelled her to wear a vibrant purple dress with a hot pink sash that showed her dark coloring and narrow waist to advantage. She even took extra time with her makeup, adding a touch of purple eye shadow and a few strokes of mascara.

When every male head turned as she walked into the lobby, she began to regret dressing with such flamboyance, but it was too late to go home and change.

"You're dressed to kill today," Walt noted dryly as he set up the equipment in the isolation booth. "I'm sure it doesn't have a thing to do with who's coming in this morning."

She sighed. "Hey, let's not get started on that."

"On what?" he asked innocently.

"Look, I don't know where you get the idea there's something between Dylan Hamlin and me. After these experiments are over, I'm going to be seeing him on a professional basis. And that means no outside involvement."

He gave a gentle tug on the hot pink sash and laughed. "I'm not as dumb as I look."

"Walt . . ."

Their conversation was interrupted when Dylan walked through the door. Sonia felt a rush of pleasure at the sight of him. He was wearing black jeans that hugged his long, muscular thighs, and a khaki shirt that set off his tan. The entire lab suddenly seemed to glow. Then it grew dim again as she saw the partner he'd brought with him.

"Dr. Barnes, Walt, this is Marlee Elden."

Walt's small eyes widened. "Hi. Weren't you on *Dallas* recently?"

Marlee nodded, delighted at being recognized. "You must be a memory expert. That was such a small role. I only had a few lines."

Sonia tended to agree with Marlee. It would have taken a memory expert to be able to distinguish this woman's blond, fresh-scrubbed, athletic looks from dozens of Hollywood clones. Advertising executives seemed to consider the type essential for selling everything from toothpaste to motorcycles.

"You been an actress long?" asked Walt, fishing for something to say to her.

"No. I just started, really. Basically, I'm a stuntwoman."

"You work with Dylan quite a bit?" said Sonia.

"I try to avoid it." Dylan tousled her blond curls playfully. "Actually, we're working on a stunt for a movie now."

"The one with the helicopter?"

"Yes," Dylan answered. "Marlee will be the girl I lift out of the back seat of the convertible."

No wonder he was so anxious to be hypnotized. It wasn't just his own neck he was worried about breaking.

Were they lovers? Sonia observed the affectionate familiarity between the two and decided it was likely.

It would be difficult to dislike Marlee. She had an easygoing California openness, an unselfconscious beauty that was worn as effortlessly as her golden tan. But as much as Sonia wanted to like her, she found herself stopped by a chilling wave of jealousy. Had Walt felt this way about Dylan?

Fortunately, Marlee seemed oblivious to Sonia's feelings and chattered to her as though they were old friends. If she saw Sonia as an adversary, she didn't show it. Either she was supremely confident in their relationship, or Dylan had never given her any reason to be jealous.

"I've had dozens of psychic experiences," Marlee told her with enthusiasm. "The weirdest things happen in my life, too weird for coincidence, you know? And especially with Dylan. He and I were in the middle of a barroom brawl scene one time. It was all choreographed out, but this one kid—he was new in the business—got carried away and was about to jump on Dylan. I opened my mouth and before I could say anything, Dylan moved out of the way. Later, he said he knew what I was thinking."

So there were other women's minds Dylan could read. It was ridiculous, but she felt as betrayed as if he'd been two-timing her.

"Well, I hope we can come up with some good results today," Sonia said pleasantly.

Leaving Marlee in Walt's more-than-willing care, Sonia accompanied Dylan to the adjoining room and watched him stretch out on the small bed. "You know the instructions, so I don't have to repeat them to you," she said as she switched on the microphone.

He grabbed her hand as she was about to leave. "Have you decided on the reward you're going to give me if I get all the right answers?"

"How about a punch in the nose?"

"Not much of an inducement."

"Do it for science."

"I'd rather do it for—"

Suppressing a smile, she yanked her hand away and closed the door before he could continue. She had to wonder if Marlee's self-confidence would be punctured if she realized her faithful lover was flirting outrageously in the next room.

Walt was happily engaged in explaining the experiment to the young actress. "You'll be shown five videotapes we hope will have an emotional impact on you. We'd like you to concentrate on transmitting them to Dylan in the next room."

"This sounds like fun," said Marlee.

"You'll love it." He winked at her.

Using Dylan's suggestion, they had not labeled the tapes and had no idea of the order in which they'd be shown. Sonia jotted down the results on the chart as each videotape came up. By the end of the session she was bursting with excitement. ESP was the factor in the first, but the second could be nothing else but precognition. Dylan had proved he could perform consistently in a laboratory environment.

He and Marlee joined them in the lab and she showed them the chart.

TRANSMITTER'S VIDEOTAPE	RECEIVER'S COMMENTS
1. Water skiing	"Foam, water splashing . . . a boat, a speedboat"
2. Astronaut floating in space	"Oceanwaves . . . no, cannons, old cannons like the Pirates of the Caribbean at Disneyland"
3. Swashbuckling scene from Errol Flynn movie SEA HAWK—pirates	"I'm seeing houses in a row, little Victorian-style houses like in San Francisco."

Looking at the result of the first one, Marlee hugged Dylan. "Hey babe, we did it! I knew you and I had ESP!"

Then she read the rest of the chart and looked up at Sonia with astonishment. "Yee gads. Does this mean what I think it does?"

"Yes," said Sonia. "While you were watching Number two, Dylan correctly predicted what would show up on Number Three. In other words, he predicted the future."

"I thought I could do better than that," said Dylan.

"Believe me, this is extraordinary enough. We're lucky sometimes even to get one instance of ESP in a laboratory experiment, and this makes twice you've been able to make a correct prediction. It's almost unheard of."

Marlee was still puzzling over the chart. "You know something, Dr. Barnes, maybe this doesn't mean anything, but both the straight ESP and the precognition had something to do with stunts. There was the water skiing and then the sword fight on that old ship for the Errol Flynn pirate movie."

"Marlee, you may have hit on something," said Sonia with growing excitement. "The other day the tapes he got right were about a roller coaster, which is close to a stunt, and the other was clowns in a circus. Both those things he could identify with closely."

"The water skiing wasn't a stunt," Walt pointed out.

"Actually, I did some stunt water skiing for a spy thriller about a year ago."

"Wasn't that the movie where you went off the cliff?" asked Marlee.

"Off a cliff?" Sonia's mouth dropped.

He laughed. "I'll bring in the sequence and you can see it. In fact, I could bring you in tapes of stunts I've done if you want to use them for the experiment."

"That would be fascinating," said Sonia. "Walt and I were trying to pick scenes that got the adrenaline going, and there's probably nothing that charges both of you up more than stunt work."

"How about some stunts I've done?" asked Marlee. "I've got a bunch of tapes you'd be welcome to use."

"Wonderful! We'll run both and see which ones have a stronger impact—the ones where the receiver is involved or where the transmitter is."

"An ESP study was done a few years ago that compared the responses of actors with those of people in other professions, and the actors generally scored higher. I'm wondering if stunt-people might have a higher capacity for precognition." Sonia was already thinking ahead to a possible study just using stuntpeople and running tapes of their stunts.

In her enthusiasm she nearly forgot about Dylan's hypnosis. "I really should ask if you'd be willing to do more experiments. It might take some time to do this, and that would mean putting off the hypnosis again."

He looked at Marlee. Obviously she weighed heavily in his decision. "If we can do the experiments soon. I don't want to postpone the hypnosis much longer."

"As soon as you get me the tapes, Walt will have them transferred onto our cassettes and we'll begin."

"I'll get them to you tomorrow."

"This is so thrilling," Marlee enthused. "It's like being in on the discovery of . . . relativity or something."

Dylan threw an arm around her. "Marlee, I've always said you were a veritable Albert Einstein."

Sonia felt a painful twist of jealousy watching Marlee and Dylan walk out the door arm in arm, discussing which tapes to bring in.

"They make a cute couple, don't they?" said Walt, gloating on her discomfort.

"A handsome couple," she said brightly, gathering up her charts.

Walt had a bone he wasn't about to give up easily. "Both of them so . . . physical, they probably have a lot in common, kind of like those two jockeys who are married."

"Having things in common makes a good basis for a relationship," she said noncommittally.

"I'm glad it didn't bother you seeing them together."

"Come on, Walt. Why should it?"

He laughed. "Kind of a waste of that dress, wasn't it?"

She felt the heat rising on her cheeks, but instead of giving vent to her anger, she smiled and said, "Well, we got some superb results today. I might be able to use them in my meeting with McCabe tomorrow. It's budget time again, and I'm dreading the inevitable confrontation."

Back in her office she thought about what Walt had said. He was right about her being affected by Marlee. She didn't dare admit how much, even to herself. She even deluded herself into thinking she was glad he was so happily attached. It set the barriers between them more firmly in place.

For the moment she had to turn all her thoughts to a strategy for keeping her budget intact. Each semester it was a fight with McCabe to maintain psychical research.

McCabe's rat experiments were respected throughout the world and he took great pride in them. But it had always been a puzzle to Sonia, even in her undergraduate days, why rats should figure so prominently in human psychology. There seemed so little correlation between rodent and human behavior. What self-respecting human would run himself ragged through a maze for a piece of cheese?

And some of the experiments, she felt, touched on the sadistic. In one study rats were dropped into a water barrel while the researcher observed how long it took them to stop struggling and drown.

"How can you sleep nights knowing that's going on in your department?" she had raged at Dr. McCabe. "It's like something devised by the Gestapo! And what possible good will that ever do humanity?"

He had eventually halted the experiment, but budget cuts in parapsychology followed, and she had been on strained terms with Dr. McCabe ever since.

She spread the charts of the recent experiment on her desk. No matter what his feelings on psychical research, McCabe would have to be impressed. Dylan Hamlin was unique, a subject who could actually predict the future in a laboratory environment.

It was going to be fascinating to see how Dylan and Marlee performed when viewing their own stunts. As she turned the variables over in her mind, she realized that what she really needed was a control team, two more stuntpeople to view the exact same tapes. It was the only way to find out if there were more instances of ESP when the videotapes were of a personal nature. That Dylan and Marlee were lovers could be an even greater factor than their being stuntpeople, although maybe it was only Dylan's psychic ability that made it work. At any rate, a control team would at least eliminate some of those questions.

Dylan probably knew some fellow stuntpeople who would cooperate. She checked her watch and wondered if he might have arrived home by now. She dialed his number and he answered on the first ring.

"Yes."

"You don't say hello?" she couldn't help teasing.

He laughed. "Okay, hello, Dr. Barnes."

"You recognized my voice, or you had a feeling it was me when you picked up the phone?"

"Both, I guess. And it's good to hear your voice. How are you?"

With some dismay she realized that even the sound of his voice over the telephone did something to her. Keep it under control, she told herself.

"I was just thinking about the next experiment. I'm going to need a control—a team to watch the same videotapes. Do you think you could find me two more stuntpeople?"

"Sure. There's my friend Quinn, the helicopter pilot. I'm sure he'd help out, and I can ask around for someone else."

"You're sure it's not too much trouble?"

"Not at all. There isn't much going on at the studios right now."

"Thanks. I really appreciate your help."

"Something's wrong," he said with concern. "You okay?"

"Fine."

"No, you're not. I can hear it in your voice."

"It's nothing, honestly." She wasn't about to admit how talking to him made her feel.

He hesitated a moment. "Is it anything to do with Walt?"

"No, everything's fine, really."

There was a brief silence; then he said, "You know that was him I saw when we first talked. . . . There's something about that guy. His feelings about you are muddled right now. There's admiration and envy and . . . well, he's kind of hung up on you besides. That could be a lethal combination. Watch out for him."

"Thanks, but I really don't think there's any

problem." Sonia felt uncomfortable about the warning. Somehow she knew he was right, but what could she do? You couldn't fire someone just because a psychic thought he was going to cause you trouble.

"Did Marlee enjoy the experiment?" she asked to change the subject.

"Hey, Marlee," he called out. "Did you enjoy the experiment?"

"It was great!" The voice sounded close-by.

The ache of jealousy returned at the thought of Marlee at his house, by his side at that moment. Did they live together?

"You're going to drop off those tapes tomorrow?" Sonia asked.

"I've got meetings lined up most of the day, but I can be by your office around five. Will you be there then?"

She glanced down quickly at her calendar. That was when she was scheduled to meet with Dr. McCabe. Maybe she could postpone the dread meeting a little longer. Seeing Dylan Hamlin was an infinitely more appealing prospect.

"Five o'clock is fine."

"Good, see you then."

As she hung up the phone she noticed that her heart was pumping faster and that her palms were damp. Bad signs.

She dialed McCabe's extension and it was busy. Then an emergency phone call came through from an attendant on a disturbed ward upstairs. One of Sonia's patients was screaming for her. "Can you get up here immediately?"

asked the attendant. Sonia assured them she would, and as she rushed through the door she nearly bumped into Walt Anguin.

"Oh, Walt, can you do me a favor?"

"Sure."

"I've got to see an emergency patient upstairs. And it may take a while. Could you call Dr. McCabe for me and tell him I have to cancel our appointment for tomorrow afternoon?"

"How come?"

"Dylan Hamlin's coming by with the tapes." The moment the words were out, she regretted it. Walt's thin lips twisted into a nasty smile.

"Of course Hamlin's infinitely more important than the head of the department."

"Look, I can't stop to explain. I've got to get upstairs. Please just make the phone call for me, will you? McCabe likes to know things at least a day in advance."

"Sure," said Walt.

She spent three grueling hours with her patient, and when she finally reached home that night she was too exhausted to eat.

Throwing herself across the bed, she closed her eyes. As soon as she was relaxed, the image of Dylan Hamlin came to her. Was there any way to get that man off her mind? She smiled and ran a hand over the pillows. Tonight, after all the turmoil, she rather welcomed the pleasant fantasies about him.

Had he actually seen the two of them there making love? Well, if he hadn't, she certainly could. In the last few days she had become obsessed with the idea. Every time she was

around him she thought about it. A tremor
came back to her when she remembered those
few moments in his arms at the racetrack.

Then she stopped herself. He was probably at
that very moment wrapped in Marlee's arms.

The following day dragged along interminably
until she was to see him at five o'clock. She
wanted to double-check with Walt to make sure
he had canceled her appointment, but he'd left a
message with her secretary saying he was at
home with the flu and when she called his
apartment there was no answer. It was a sunny,
warm day. He had probably gone to the beach—
Southern California students tended to do that.
Just to be sure McCabe knew about the cancel-
lation, she dialed his office, but the line was
busy and she decided it was silly to worry.
Whatever she had asked Walt to do, he had
always gotten on it immediately. His dependa-
bility was one of the things that had made him
invaluable to her.

When Dylan finally walked into her office, she
found it was all she could do to keep her nerves
under control. All the vivid fantasies from the
night before came rushing back to her.

He placed a stack of videotape cassettes on
her desk and said, "How's it going?"

"Fine. And you?" Why did he make her feel
like a teenager on her first date?

He gazed at her for a long moment, his eyes
partially hooded. "I'm all right."

"No recurrence of the nightmare?"

"Not last night."

Was that because Marlee had been with him? she wondered. An awkward silence hung between them as they gazed at each other steadily.

"Do you want to look at the tapes now?" he said finally.

"The video cassette recorder is all locked up. I'll wait until tomorrow when Walt's here to do the transferring."

He noticed some Kirlian photographs on her desk. "You doing research on solar flares?"

"Believe it or not, those are photos of people's fingertips."

He examined the pictures more closely. "What's all this colored flame-like stuff and bubbles shooting out from them?"

"We're not sure. There are a million theories. One is that it's an invisible substance called bioplasma, effluvium or orgone. Some Eastern religions talk about *chi* or *prana*. I've heard psychics talk about a life force or an energy body . . ."

"An energy body?" He looked amused.

"Supposedly, it's a kind of aura that surrounds the body. In the Middle Ages, artists painted gold halos around the heads of saints. A lot of psychics claim to have seen them around people. You never have?"

"No, though I can't say I've ever looked for it. How did you get these photographs?"

"It's a complicated mechanism. I'm not sure I understand it fully. A Russian couple named Kirlian invented it back in the forties. It involves taking pictures using high-frequency electricity fields."

She handed him a bulging file folder that contained hundreds of Kirlian photographs. "This is Walt's finger pad in a normal state. See the regular corona around it?" She showed him another picture. "And here's where he got himself worked into an angry state." The colors had changed to hues of red and the corona was irregular. "Emotions and even the state of health can change it drastically."

Dylan was fascinated. "What happens when you take a Kirlian photograph of two people together?"

"Strange things." She pulled out another file folder. This is Walt and me in a relaxed state. Both coronas are normal. Now, here's where we made strong eye contact."

"Only one finger shows up," said Dylan with amazement.

"We've found that when eye contact is made there's always one person who dominates and eclipses the other."

"Which aura disappeared?"

"Walt's."

"I thought that would be the case."

She didn't want to get on the dangerous subject of Walt. "I've done a lot of studies with families. Look at this one. It's a mother, father, daughter and son."

"But there are only three finger pads."

"Right. It turned out the teenage son was rebelling and having problems in the family, and his finger pad totally disappeared."

"Are you sure those flares aren't caused by body heat?"

"Temperature has nothing to do with it; nor does moisture, though we can get different effects by varying the amount of electricity."

She showed him another. "This one's interesting. It's a mother, father and their six-year-old child. The auras of the mother and father overlap, and auras of the mother and the son overlap. But there is a blank space between the child and the father. It's exactly what Freud might have predicted for that age."

"Do you have this equipment set up now?"

"It's in the lab. Why?"

"I'm curious to see what happens when you and I have our finger pads taken."

Sonia was curious too. Would their attraction show up on film? Would Dylan dominate her to the point where her aura disappeared? Though she had done hundreds of "family portraits," she'd never done anything with couples who had a romantic attraction. Perhaps a better test would be to bring in Marlee, but it was too good an opportunity to pass up at the moment.

"You want to try it?"

"By all means."

They went into the lab and Sonia first took some pictures of his finger pads alone. She developed them immediately. "There must be something wrong," she said worriedly. "I'm not getting any image of you."

She tried some pictures of her own finger pads. Hers showed up clearly, so it was not the equipment.

"I wonder what would happen if I put myself in a trancelike state," Dylan said.

"Try it," she suggested.

He closed his eyes and relaxed. As soon as she saw his eyelids flutter, she took the picture. This one came out, the corona as vivid as any.

"It's very strange," she said, shaking her head. "Let's try the two of us together making eye contact."

She sat down beside him on the bench. They were touching shoulders as they placed their fingers on the photographic plate. The moment she caught his direct gaze, she felt a tremor pass through her, and at that moment she pressed the button with her other hand.

Sonia had been expecting his corona to dominate and eclipse hers, but both showed brightly in reds and oranges, flaring slightly at each other and intermeshing.

"I wonder what would happen if we kissed," he said.

"Uh, that's not very scientific."

"Why not? Have you ever taken one of two people kissing?"

"No, I've never thought of it."

"You've got to admit it's one of the most emotionally charged things two people can do."

"You're right about that." Her voice was beginning to sound breathless. "It's just that it's so . . ." From a purely scientific standpoint, he was right. And from a personal standpoint, every nerve in her body was dying for it. No, she couldn't kiss Dylan. It was utterly unethical . . . and yet, to be honest with herself, it was utterly desired.

His turquoise eyes were challenging, drawing her into him.

"All right, she said after a moment. "To my knowledge this was never been done before with Kirlian photography."

"Just the sort of stunt that appeals to me," he said slowly. While leaving his finger pad on the photographic plate, he took her face in his other hand, lightly caressing her cheek, running his thumb over her lips.

With one hand on the remote button and the other on the plate, she felt helpless and giddy as she closed her eyes and felt his lips come down on hers. They were softer than she had imagined, moving in a whisper, urging her mouth open.

This was more kiss than she'd bargained for. For a scientific experiment it had really lasted long enough, but she was reluctant to give up the wonderful feeling.

They played and parried with their mouths and tongues until she sternly reminded herself of the purpose and pressed the remote button.

It was at that moment she heard the lab door open. Breaking away from Dylan quickly, she turned to see Dr. McCabe.

"Dr. Barnes?" He managed to draw out the single-syllable name into three.

Standing up and busying herself with the film, she forced a calm tone of voice. "Hello, Dr. McCabe. I'd like to introduce Dylan Hamlin. He's volunteered for some experiments with us."

"May I ask what sort of experiment you're doing? Or is it altogether obvious?"

She straightened her back. "I'm doing Kirlian photography, and we were trying different emotional reactions—"

"Oh, is that what they're calling it nowadays? It's not hard to see why you so carelessly forgot your appointment with me this afternoon."

She had a sinking feeling. "Didn't Walt Anguin call you yesterday and tell you I had to cancel?"

"No, he did not. Does this important research engage so much of your time that you can't call and cancel your own appointments?"

"I received an emergency call yesterday afternoon and—"

"Dr. Barnes," McCabe interrupted her, "I must remind you that the University of Los Angeles is a dignified institution, that this hospital is one of the most highly respected psychiatric facilities in the world. Lab space is at a premium around here. Important work needs to be done, and I have to turn down requests so that you can play around like this. I cannot countenance this kind of frivolous behavior."

"Dr. McCabe, I would suggest we make another appointment for Monday and we discuss this fully then."

"I'm free at ten o'clock," he said, then added sarcastically, "Nice to have met you, Mr. Hamlin."

"Why do I get the feeling he didn't mean that?" Dylan said after McCabe left. "I hope this didn't get you into trouble."

"Not any more than I'm already in with him. Well, let's see how the photograph turned out," she said to lighten the situation.

"Is that the guy you call Rat?"

"How'd you guess?" She developed the film and held it up to the light. "Wow, look at this!"

The photo showed sparks shooting off in every direction, bubbling, linking and twining together in a garish rainbow of colors. If she could have painted a picture of how it felt to kiss Dylan Hamlin, this would have been it. It was almost worth having angered McCabe.

"Shall we try it again and see if we get the same result?" Dylan asked her.

"No, I think once was enough."

"But I thought the key word in a scientific experiment was *repeatable*. Don't you need to build up some more statistics? What if that was just a fluke?"

She hated to admit it, but he was right. "Okay, just one more." Her voice was a little more unsteady than she would have liked.

She placed her finger next to Dylan's on the photographic plate and leaned toward him.

He was in no hurry this time to complete the kiss. Instead, he looked down at her for a long moment, a smile playing at the corners of his mouth. His free hand caressed her neck and dropped lower, almost touching her breast. "Funny, I never thought I had much aptitude for science," he said softly.

Her lips parted in anticipation as his face neared. She closed her eyes and was surprised to feel his lips lightly graze her eyebrows and eyelids, the tip of her nose and her cheeks. He knew she wouldn't take the picture until he had reached her lips, and he was purposely trying to prolong it. But she didn't have the heart to protest. It was all too pleasant to let him continue.

His fingers lightly caressed the tip of her breast, and she felt the nipple grow taut as the flames shot through her. She was generating so much voltage that she doubted they even needed the machine. Those sparks and flares would probably show up on the photographic plate without it. Still he put off the actual kiss until the agony of waiting became unbearable.

When their lips finally meshed together, she pressed the button. There was no reason to continue the kiss and yet she wasn't sure she could stop it—or even if she wanted to. It took all her willpower to pull away from him.

Standing abruptly and avoiding his eyes, she busied herself with developing the film.

The coronas on this picture were even more vivid than the last, reflecting all the turbulence that existed between them.

"This was certainly interesting," she said uneasily.

"Most," he agreed. "Why don't we go get a drink somewhere?"

"Oh, I don't think so."

"Why not?"

"Because it's—"

"Socializing with a patient?"

"Yes."

"Forget I'm a patient and just think of me as a laboratory experiment."

"It's highly unethical, unorthodox and unprofessional, and—"

"What we just did probably falls somewhere in there too. Having a drink together won't make it any worse."

"It won't make it any better either." She glanced down at her trembling hands. "I don't know why I always find myself being talked into things by you. First it was the ESP experiment; then you bullied me into letting you make bets at the track. And now . . ."

"Are you sorry you let me bully you into those kisses?"

The electric glow of sensations rushed back into her. "In all honesty, no."

"I'm glad you're honest, Sonia, because where we're headed, we're going to have to be honest with each other."

"The only place I can see we're headed is out to get a drink."

He grinned down at her. "For the moment."

Chapter 5

THE LATE-AFTERNOON SKY WAS STREAKED WITH vermilion, and the slanting sunbeams bathed the weathered brick campus buildings in misty golden light. The university had been founded in the late 1800s during the Spanish architectural revival, and through the years, planners had been careful to maintain the essence of its Spanish charm with shady arcades, flowered courtyards and tiled fountains.

Sonia squinted up at the fiery setting sun and the carnival-colored sky. "Say what you want about the smog in L.A.," said Sonia, "but you have to admit it gives us spectacular sunsets."

"I'd rather give up the sunsets and be able to breathe," said Dylan. He plucked a yellow daisy and handed it to her. "This is a nice campus. Did you do your undergraduate work here?"

"The last two years. I started out at Berkeley."

"Is that where you're from originally?"

"Nearby."

"What brought you to Southern California?"

"I came down here for a visit, expecting to hate it. We're so brainwashed up there into thinking of L.A. as Tinsel Town. There's some of that, of course, but this campus won me over. And the people were so open and friendly. You can't imagine the culture shock to have people smiling at you for no reason at all. On the Berkeley campus everyone's too wrapped up in their own little high-pressured worlds to take the time to smile."

"It's not easy to smile when you're not happy," said Dylan.

"Or in competition with everyone else. What brought you to Los Angeles, the circus?"

"The movie business. My army buddy, Quinn, the pilot I told you about, had lived here all his life and had some industry contacts. He said, what the hell, we might as well get paid for doing stunts we were doing in Vietnam for nothing. I was planning to return to the circus, but figured I'd give this a try for a few months. Then one morning I woke up and found I'd been here for ten years."

They walked through the Student Park under sycamore and maple trees. Bright pink and red azalea bushes were in full bloom. Sonia took a deep breath. In spite of the collision with Dr. McCabe, she felt wonderfully alive and content walking beside Dylan. The blue shadows of dusk made the sculptured planes of his face even more dramatic and had turned the shade of his eyes a deep midnight blue.

"So you don't think we're headed toward an affair?" he asked with amusement.

"No, I don't. And I don't think we should even discuss it."

"I thought you shrinks like to talk everything out."

"That may be true, but this is one subject I think we're safer avoiding for the moment. Where do you pick up your information about shrinks? Have you ever been to see one?"

"In the army once. Some of these psychic experiences can be pretty strange. I wanted to talk to a doctor about them. He didn't believe in any of it, told me the famous psychoanalyst Carl Jung had investigated it and declared it all bunk. How did you get started researching it? Did you ever have any psychic experiences?"

"None, but when I was doing graduate work, I happened to pick up a copy of the *Journal of the American Society of Psychical Research* and was fascinated. Before I knew it, I was hooked."

They reached the end of the park and walked through the brick campus gates that led into the ULA Center. It was a charming village of tree-lined streets filled with sidewalk cafés, movie theaters, boutiques and bookstores. At any time of the day or night, it was a lively place.

As they passed one of the movie theaters, he looked up at the marquee. "That's the movie where I did that water-skiing stunt."

"The one where you went off the cliff?"

"Here's the scene." He pointed to the place on

the poster that showed the skiers racing toward the cliff.

"It looks like one of those superspy thrillers."

"God love them. They keep food on the table."

"It's embarrassing to admit, but I don't think I've ever even seen a James Bond movie."

"That takes guts to admit. It's un-American not to like spy thrillers. But then, Walt was saying you don't go to movies at all."

"I'm not fanatic about it. There are some movies I like."

"What kind?"

"European movies, where the concentration is on the psychological violence people do to each other rather than the physical."

"That kind of violence can be just as deadly," said Dylan thoughtfully.

"The sort of thing that keeps food on *my* table."

She looked closely at the movie poster. "Was this you leaping over alligators?"

He laughed. "It sure wasn't the star. He was scared to death of the slimy critters."

"And you weren't?"

"They gave me a few tense moments, but we had their feet anchored down at the bottom of the pond so they couldn't move around."

She had a sudden inspiration. "Listen, rather than have a drink, let's go in and see the film and then you can explain to me how you do the stunts. It would give me a much better idea of what exactly your work is and it might make it easier for me to help you under hypnosis."

"Tell you what, I'll forfeit my drink if you

promise to have dinner with me afterward while I explain the stunts to you."

"You're on."

They had an argument at the ticket booth since Sonia insisted on paying her own way. "Come on, Dylan. This isn't a date."

"But it's my movie."

"Then you'll have to let me treat you to dinner," she insisted.

With his hand on the small of her back, he steered her into the movie theater. "We'll cross those alligators when we come to them."

Sonia was prepared to be bored with the movie, but from the first scene she was caught up in the action. The dialogue, the plot and the women's costumes might have been scanty, but the stunts, which made up most of the movie, were breathtaking.

The opening sequence was shot on a ski slope. The spy, in a black ski mask, was being chased down the hill by two villains. As the camera pulled back, the wide expanse revealed a sheer cliff. At any minute she was certain he'd turn, but he kept going until he was flying off it.

Sonia gripped Dylan's arm in terror and whispered, "Is that you?"

He wrapped his fingers around her hand. "Yes. Watch this. It's a hell of a stunt."

She could barely stand to watch, peeking out between the fingers that covered her eyes. It was worse than any roller coaster ride. Dylan was sailing off a steep cliff in midair, and beneath him was a lake. The two villains stopped at the edge of the cliff and shook their heads.

Gently Dylan removed the fingers from her eyes. "Here comes the good part."

Suddenly a parachute opened and Dylan floated down to the lake. Sonia wondered what would happen when the parachute hit the water. It would have to weigh him down and pull him under. But just as he was about to touch the surface, he threw out a grappling hook that attached to a speedboat cutting through the water. He hit a buckle that threw off the parachute and calmly began to water-ski behind the boat.

Sonia swallowed hard. "I can't believe you did that!"

He chuckled. "Neither did the director. He thought the shot was impossible, and we managed to do it in one take."

The film progressed from one death-defying stunt to another. In the alligator scene, the hero had been dropped off on a concrete island in the center of a pond teeming with hungry alligators. She couldn't see where it made a difference knowing they were anchored down. The huge jaws were snapping, the tails lashing out. Dylan blithely used their backs as stepping stones, leaping from one to the next to make the escape.

In the final scene a car flew off a broken bridge, spiraled in midair and landed on four wheels at the other side of the river.

Sonia was aghast. "Were you driving that car?"

"Yes. Good effect, wasn't it?"

She wondered why she'd ever been worried

about a few lane changes on the freeway. By the time she walked out of the movie house, she was drained. Everyone else, she noticed, had had a wonderfully entertaining time.

"Dylan, you can't tell me those stunts weren't dangerous."

"It looks worse than it is. We take a lot of precautions."

"Like tying down the alligators? Big deal. Those toothy jaws were still loose. What if you'd fallen in the pond?"

"I did, a couple of times."

"Good Lord!"

"The problem was traction. I didn't realize how slippery the back of an alligator could be. I was dressed like the hero in a suit and tie and regular street shoes. After I slipped a couple of times, I got wise and ordered some specially prepared soles for the shoes. Then I had a problem because alligators are damn smart and it didn't take them long to figure out what I was going to do. By the time we got to the last take, they had their jaws open just waiting for me to slip and fall in."

They stopped at a charming Italian restaurant and were shown to a table in the center of the room. Dylan frowned his disapproval. "We'd prefer something more private where we can sit side by side. How about the booth in the corner over there?"

"I'm sorry, sir, but that one's reserved."

"It was," said Dylan. With a move as slick as a magician's, he slipped some bills into the hostess's palm. Sonia was amused to see the woman quickly change direction and lead them to the corner booth.

Dylan Hamlin was obviously used to getting his own way and didn't seem to mind how he got it.

When the Chianti arrived, he lifted his wine glass in a toast. "Here's to science."

Reminded of the kiss in the lab, she flushed and averted her eyes as she sipped the wine. Her flustered reaction seemed to amuse him, for he gently pressed his thigh up against hers under the table. She would have moved away, but drawing attention to it would only be more embarrassing.

"This wine is delicious," she declared, determined to change the subject. "It's beginning to unfrazzle my nerves after that movie. It's still hard for me to understand why someone would ski off a cliff. I don't suppose it's just for the money."

"Don't knock the incentive. For that particular stunt I was paid fifty thousand dollars."

The waiter brought the antipasto, and Sonia took an olive. "You could offer me a million dollars and it wouldn't be enough."

"It's not like somebody hands you the money, you get on a pair of skis and zip off the mountain. We spent ten days at the site setting up cameras and waiting for the right weather. Just when we thought we had it, clouds would move in and obscure the mountain. Actually, what I did was less difficult than flying the helicopter that held the cameraman."

"Was that friend of yours from Vietnam piloting?"

"Yes, he's probably the best in the movie business. I don't know if I'd have agreed to do the helicopter stunt that's coming up if they'd been using anyone but Quinn. You'll meet him next week when he comes in to do the experiment. The tough thing for him in that ski stunt was keeping the helicopter a decent distance from the cliff face so that the wind from the rotor wouldn't interfere with my parachute."

She buttered a slice of fresh, warm bread. "But weren't you scared at all when you went sailing off that cliff?"

He smiled. "You'd have to be crazy not to be scared."

"You'd have to be a little crazy to do it."

"Maybe, but the feeling of sailing off that cliff was like nothing I'd ever experienced before. Doing something like that well is worth everything."

"Even your life?"

He waved away the thought. "Life is full of risks. People choke on chicken bones and die."

She wondered if he'd said that just because she'd ordered the chicken parmigiana. "Did you have any premonitions of impending disaster about that stunt?"

"No, just the normal fear."

"Most people never experience that kind of fear in a lifetime."

He took her hand between his and gazed intently into her eyes. "You're wrong, Sonia. Most people experience fear every day. But it's fear of losing their jobs or their hair. They fear growing old, or that they'll say the wrong thing at a party. And those little fears whittle away at them, giving them ulcers and heart attacks that destroy them just as easily as the things I do."

"You're talking about stress, which can be controlled. And that still doesn't answer why you do that kind of work."

"What do you think are my reasons?"

"I don't know. That's why I'm asking you." Sonia wondered if he was ready to open up and decided to give it a try. "Why don't we start with what made you decide to leave home?"

"The same reason you left Berkeley: to find something better."

He was evading again, but the main course arrived and for the moment she let the subject drop as she ate her chicken parmigiana.

"A thirteen-year-old running away from home must have had a damn good reason," she began again after a moment.

His jaw tightened. "Thirteen-year-olds run away from home all the time. Go down to Hollywood. The streets are full of them. I was lucky the circus took me. A kid couldn't ask for a better home."

"But why did you leave the one you had?"

He gave her a stony look. "Hey, shrink, forget you're on duty for a while."

"Don't think of it as a professional question."

"Then what is it?" he shot back.

"Curiosity about you."

His eyes narrowed dangerously. "All right, how about telling me everything that happened that day to your little brother. Then we'll discuss why I ran away from home."

He had effectively put the subject in perspective. Whatever his childhood had been, it was too painful for dinner conversation. He probably kept it as carefully locked away as she did her brother's death. Whatever it was, it held the key not only to why he skied off cliffs, but to the nightmares that haunted him.

"All right," she said lightly. "I want to hear more about your stunts. Tell me how they got that car to spiral off that bridge."

"We hired some aerospace engineers and had them work out the mathematical aspects on a computer; then we had a special ramp constructed . . ." He stopped and took a sip of Chianti. "No, enough talk about stunts, about me. I want to know about Dr. Sonia Barnes."

"I suppose it's only fair. What would you like to know?"

"Have you ever been in love?"

"No."

"It didn't take you long to answer that one."

Like many psychologists trained to focus on a patient, she was uncomfortable talking about herself. "There's not much to say on the subject. I've been involved with men, but the big 'L' has always eluded me."

"Why?"

She looked away from his penetrating eyes. "I suppose if I knew, it wouldn't elude me."

"You've never talked to a shrink about it?" he teased.

"Why love works or why it doesn't may be just as mysterious as why we have auras."

He ran a caressing hand over her cheek and turned her face gently toward him. "You don't want to talk about it, do you?"

"Have you ever been in love?"

"That's a tricky way to get out of an answer."

"Have you?"

"Yes."

Was he going to tell her about Marlee? She hoped not. Marlee Elden was the last person she wanted to inject into the conversation. Sonia could have killed herself for even bringing it up.

A curtain of silence suddenly descended between them. Sonia, for all her professional expertise, wasn't sure how to tear it down or even if she wanted to. She usually had no trouble talking to people. Part of her talent in psychology was in getting people to talk about themselves, but with Dylan their conversations seemed to be studded with these awkward moments of silence.

Words churned around in her brain, words that expressed all her raging feelings for him, but that wasn't something she could talk about either. Nor did she want to discuss his girlfriend. But as a psychologist, she was disturbed by that. How was she going to get through to him about those nightmares if she couldn't bear to hear him talk about the woman he loved and who was involved in the same dangerous stunt. Never before had the fine line between professional and personal relationships been so blurred for her.

"I'm crazy about Italian food," she said, deciding for the moment to switch to safe, neutral ground.

He seemed just as relieved. "You ever been to Italy?"

"Just once. I didn't care for it."

"Why not?"

"The men."

He gave her a quizzical smile. "What about the men?"

"They don't leave you alone for a minute. Italians produce the best-looking men in the world, and probably the most obnoxious."

Dylan threw back his head and laughed. "Would it make any difference to you to know that I was Italian?"

"With a name like Dylan?"

"Actually, I'm only half Italian. My mother was from Palermo. I was born Mario, but I changed it when I joined the circus."

"To have a stage name?"

"No. So that my father couldn't find me."

This was the first real mention of his parents and she was dying to pursue it, but something in his eyes told her to let it ride for the moment. "How did you come up with Dylan Hamlin?"

"I liked Bob Dylan songs and I had read that his real name wasn't Dylan either, so it seemed like a good name to borrow. And Hamlin was because of the Pied Piper of Hamlin. The circus for me was like the Pied Piper. I went to a performance one afternoon and watched a guy on a trapeze do a triple somersault. It was the most breathtaking thing I'd ever seen. And I decided right there that it was what I wanted to do."

"And you've been doing breathtaking things ever since."

He smiled nostalgically. "I joined up expecting to fly through the air with the greatest of ease and be hounded by beautiful women in sequined costumes. But the first few years they have you paying your dues taking care of the animals. I found I loved the horses and got started doing acrobatics with an Italian family of equestrian stars. Later I worked my way into trapeze flying."

"And then you were chased by sequined women?"

"Contrary to popular belief, circus girls are kept under tighter reins than most. You fool around with them and you've got their brothers, fathers and uncles breathing down your neck. You never had any fantasies about running off to join the circus?"

"It's funny," she mused. "When I was a kid I used to hang upside down in an old oak tree in front of our house and imagine I was on a trapeze. I loved the circus, but I haven't been to one in years and years."

"Then I'll have to take you. Barnum and Bailey will be in town next month. In fact, you should come out to my house. I've got a trapeze all set up. I'll put a harness on you and you can try it."

She was aghast. "Are you kidding? Dylan, I'd be terrified!"

"Not if I started you out slowly. Marlee didn't

know a thing two months ago, and now she doesn't even use a harness. I've been teaching her some trapeze work so she'll get used to grasping on to my wrists for that stunt."

"But Marlee is a stuntwoman—she's essentially a professional athlete. She's used to doing things like that. I can barely put one foot in front of the other without tripping. Get me up on a trapeze and I'd break my neck. I know my limits."

He took her hand and traced sensuously around her fingers slowly, watching her eyes. "Dr. Sonia Barnes, I don't think you have any idea what your limits are."

Her mouth was dry as the sensations shot through her. She suddenly recalled one of McCabe's rat experiments. Having located the pleasure center in the rat's brain, he had attached electrodes to it. The sensation was evidently so excruciatingly wonderful that the little rodent pushed a lever again and again to activate it until he dropped of exhaustion. Sonia had a feeling making love to Dylan Hamlin would be something like that.

"Come by my place tomorrow, then—it's Saturday. You can watch us work. I think you'd enjoy it."

She wasn't wildly enthusiastic about watching him fly through the air with Marlee Elden, but having the opportunity to see how he lived and to watch him at work would be a great help in understanding him better.

"In fact, my buddy Quinn is coming over," he added, "and we'll be working out a fight scene we're doing for a shoot on Monday. You'll see exactly how we go about making something look dangerous when it really isn't."

"I wouldn't be in the way?"

"Not at all." He wrote down the address and directions.

When the check came, she made a grab for it. "It's only fair, Dylan. We made a deal."

"What deal?"

"You paid for the movie, so I'm paying for dinner."

"Nonsense." He took the check from her. "That's all very liberated and I respect you for it, but I invited you, so it's my treat. When you invite me to dinner at your house, that'll be your treat."

There was no way she'd have him over to dinner. They'd already gone further than she knew was wise. Even going out to his house tomorrow was pushing good sense, though she could rationalize it in a professional way by her need to know more about him. Of course, what she was really curious about was if Marlee was actually living there. Rather than coming out and asking him directly, this was a perfect way to find out.

They walked slowly back through the village to the hospital parking lot. It was a warm night, with a slight breeze that ruffled the leaves of the trees along the main street. Throngs of students crowded the sidewalks, laughing and sharing their joyful student mixture of gossip and worldly profundities. Sonia thought wistfully that even in her own student days she'd never known the giddy playfulness of most college co-eds. The tragedy that had dominated her childhood had cut wounds too deep. She had worked hard at becoming well adjusted, and yet it had always seemed like asking too much to hope that she could ever be lighthearted as well. But tonight was different. Walking beside Dylan made her feel young and delightfully foolish.

And protected. There were nights she walked out to the dimly lit parking lot and was afraid. There were too many reports of campus crime, crazies lurking behind the bushes. There was a power in Dylan's broad shoulders and the feline assurance of his walk. Not many thugs would tangle with a man like that.

When they reached her car, he placed his strong hands on her shoulders and turned her toward him. "I enjoyed being with you tonight, Sonia."

"Dylan . . ."

His head was inclining toward hers, his voice husky. "I just want to finish what we started back there in the lab."

"No, we—"

His lips on hers halted any protest and for the moment suspended all rational thought. Her arms seemed to wrap around his neck of their own volition, and her fingers ran through his thick black hair.

The electricity surged through her, increasing the longer she was pressed up against him. His lips moved down her neck and he licked lightly at the pulse beneath her collarbone. The large, strong hands splayed across her hips and pressed her tighter against him.

She caught her breath and with a great effort came to her senses. Placing the palms of her hands firmly on his chest, she pushed him away.

"Good night, Dylan."

He could easily have kept her pinned to him, but he released her, opened her car door and helped her in. "Bring your bathing suit tomorrow."

She nodded.

"And drive safely."

That wouldn't be easy. Her hands were shaking so badly she could barely get the key in the ignition. Could they arrest you for driving under the influence of a kiss?

As Sonia backed her car out of the parking place, someone just in front of her switched on headlights and started a motor. It wasn't until the car pulled out just ahead of her and was directly under the streetlamp that she recognized who it was.

How long had Walt been there? Sonia couldn't remember hearing the sound of a car door opening; but then, she had blanked out everything for the few moments of the kiss. Had he been waiting there for her?

She suddenly thought about McCabe's surprise visit to her lab. If he thought she had forgotten an appointment, he would have been angry, but he wouldn't have come looking for her. Somebody had to have told him she was in the lab with Dylan. It wasn't her secretary; she had already gone home for the night by the time Dylan arrived. Walt must have been spying on her.

Her cheeks grew hot with rage, yet she was helpless to do anything. Accusing Walt of treachery could only make it worse. And she couldn't very well fire him. Tattletales might be pariahs in a schoolroom, but McCabe would be grateful for having been informed of any unorthodox behavior by his staff.

She saw Dylan's black Mustang Cobra in her rearview mirror. It was eerie that he had been able to predict trouble before he even met Walt. But then, Dylan had been the catalyst that had brought it on.

Eerie or not, she had to find some way of dealing with Walt. Now that he'd involved McCabe, the future of her research, possibly even her job, hung by a tenuous thread.

Chapter 6

SONIA HAD NEVER BEEN TO THE FAR NORTH OF the San Fernando Valley. She followed the Simi Freeway beyond the tract homes, chain stores and shopping malls to where the scenery became wild and untamed, with dramatic outcroppings of rock and rugged fields of shimmering wild mustard blossoms undulating like ocean waves in the desert wind.

Turning right at the end of the off ramp, she counted four signals, then took the first dirt road to the left, marked by a red and white striped mailbox.

A half mile up was a tan ranch-style house with white shutters. The landscaping was bare aside from a few yuccas near the front door and a sprawling rose bush that had probably never known pruning shears.

Dylan's black Cobra was parked in the driveway, and next to it was a powder blue Camaro. Marlee's? Once again she had second thoughts about coming out there, but it was too late to turn back.

Since she wasn't at work, she had felt free to dress in her normal flamboyant manner and had worn a scarlet jumpsuit with a wide parrot green belt. Bright colors always made her feel good, and knowing she looked striking gave her confidence. She'd need all she could muster to deal with the sight of Dylan and Marlee together in a cozy domestic atmosphere.

He had told her not to bother ringing the doorbell as he'd probably be in the back setting up equipment, so she walked around the side of the house and went through the gate.

The "backyard" took her by surprise. It was as though Barnum and Bailey had set up shop without the tent. There was a trapeze, a high wire, a garish cannon she supposed someone could be shot out of, a trampoline and a large swimming pool. Along one side there were even brightly painted carnival booths. Did he miss the circus so much that he felt compelled to re-create one in his own backyard?

Dylan was by the trapeze, setting some poles in place. She was about to start toward him when Marlee popped out of the back door and waved at her. She was dressed in a light peach leotard with powder blue leg warmers. The softly understated pastel outfit made Sonia suddenly feel garish in her stoplight red jumpsuit.

"Hi, Sonia," Marlee called. "I see you found your way out to this godforsaken place okay."

"Thanks to the red and white striped mailbox."

Marlee laughed. "That was my inspiration. I have no sense of direction and kept making the wrong turns."

"This is quite a setup," Sonia said, motioning around the lot. "I had no idea."

Marlee placed her hands on her narrow hips. "Isn't this a kick in the pants? The first time I saw it you could have knocked me over with a feather. A small tent circus folded a few years ago and Dylan bought a lot of their stuff cheap. Now every couple of months, when some of his old circus buddies are in town, Dylan brings busloads of underprivileged kids out here and they do a whole circus show—without the elephants and wild animals, of course. It's really fun. We have hot dogs and popcorn and cotton candy—the works. Hey, can I get you a cup of coffee or anything?"

"Oh, no thanks," Sonia answered. "I understand you're learning the trapeze."

"What a ball," she enthused. "I'm hoping to get it together well enough so I can perform for Dylan's next show here."

They began walking toward the trapeze. "You got that thing set up yet?" Marlee shouted at him.

"Just about."

Dylan finished with the final pole. He was wearing a faded black sweatshirt with the arms cut out, and she saw fully for the first time the powerful muscles of his arms. "Glad you could make it," he said, clasping her hand. All the tingles she had come to expect from his touch raced through her. "Have a seat. Marlee and I are going to go through some basic routines."

She sat down on a bench and watched them climb up opposite ladders. At the top they pulled the trapezes to them with hooks. Dylan's long body whipped the air as he swung out. After a moment he drew his knees up and over the bar and dropped his head down. Sonia's mouth grew dry and her stomach flip-flopped as she watched him swing back and forth hanging upside down. It was such an unnatural position, and yet he looked perfectly at home, calmly giving instructions to his attentive pupil.

At a signal from him, Marlee swung out, and Sonia, craning her neck, watched the dizzying swaying back and forth. She'd never sat ringside at a circus and hadn't realized how high off the ground they were.

At another signal from Dylan, Marlee let go of her trapeze, flipped around and caught Dylan's wrists.

"How was it?" she asked him.

"Your timing was a little off. Let's try it again."

Marlee nodded, dropped into the net and climbed back up the ladder. After listening to a more detailed critique of her timing and position, which Dylan delivered still hanging upside down, she swung out again.

Sonia was struck with admiration for the young woman. The soft pastels and big blue eyes were misleading. This woman had nerves of steel. For Sonia, just thinking about the climb up that rope ladder gave her goose bumps. She watched them repeat the transfer several times until Dylan was satisfied with her work.

"How'd it look from here?" Marlee asked Sonia breathlessly when she was back on the ground.

"Magnificent!"

"Oh, no," Marlee moaned. "You're too kind. I'm just glad Dylan is teaching me. He's so patient, and no matter how I bungle it, he always manages to catch me. As long as he's there I feel secure. There isn't another person in the world I'd do that helicopter stunt with."

Dylan dropped onto the net and flipped effortlessly over the side onto the ground. "You ready to try it, Sonia?"

"Oh, sure. My knees got rubbery just watching you from here."

"I'll put a harness on you so you don't have to worry about falling."

"Really, Sonia, why don't you try it?" Marlee urged. "It's so much fun."

"No thanks. Abject fear is not my idea of a good time." She turned to Dylan. "I love your backyard big top."

"It's a good place to try out new ideas for stunts," he said. They were walking past the area where a tightrope was set up. "You ever walked a tightrope?"

"They say dealing with Dr. McCabe is something like that."

"I could tell." He took her hand. "Come on, I've got one lower to the ground."

"No, Dylan, I really—"

"Try it, Sonia," said Marlee. "There's nothing dangerous. We'll put down cushions and Dylan will guide you."

Even though the tightrope was only about three feet off the ground, and there were heavy cushions under it, Sonia was still hesitant. But she had to show some guts. After all, if Marlee could swing from a trapeze, she could at least try *this*.

Dylan helped her up onto the wire and kept strong hold of her hand. "Don't worry, I'll keep you balanced."

Sonia took one tentative step and felt herself sway to the side, but Dylan's steadying arm kept her centered. He was grinning at her. "You're doing fine. Keep going." No wonder Marlee was crazy about him. He was a wonderfully patient teacher. She felt a surge of confidence.

When Sonia made it to the other end without falling, Marlee applauded. "He'll have you up there on the trapeze in no time. You just watch. Dylan has this way of seducing you into attempting things you never thought in a million years you'd do."

Sonia could well imagine. "I'm not getting on a trapeze. Nobody's that seductive."

"That's what they all say until they meet Romeo Hamlin," said a raucous voice behind them.

Sonia turned and saw a small, wiry man

about Dylan's age. He had a tattoo on one arm and an easy smile but Sonia figured that by the looks of him it wouldn't fool anyone into trying to cross him.

Marlee came forward to take Quinn's arm. "Come meet Sonia. She's the one conducting those experiments in ESP we told you about."

"Pleased to meet you. They've got me hooked into this ESP thing next week. I don't know how I'll do. I've never experienced any of that spook stuff in my life."

"You might surprise yourself," said Sonia.

"How'd you do today, kid?" he asked Marlee.

"How'd I do?" she answered turning the question over to Dylan, who threw an arm around her and gave her a kiss on the cheek.

"She did beautifully. The trampoline work yesterday really seemed to help."

Sonia's insides twisted at the warm look of affection in his eyes when he gazed at Marlee. She had to redouble the effort to keep a smile on her face so that nobody would guess her real feelings. Had she known it would be this bad, she would never have consented to come today.

Their easy physical familiarity made her feel like an intruder. And recalling the kisses from last night, she was struck through the heart with a pang of jealousy and some anger. What right did he have to come on to her when he was obviously wrapped up in Marlee? Was he one of those men who needed to conquer every female in sight?

"You guys going to rehearse some car hits for that shoot on Monday?" Marlee asked.

"Right now," said Dylan. "You want to do a few?"

"I haven't tried any in a long time. I should do some just to keep in shape."

"There's not much you need to keep in shape," said Quinn with a laugh.

Marlee changed into jeans, and all three of them attached padding to their arms and legs. "I wish I could use padding on a set," confided Marlee, "but they usually want stuntwomen in short skirts and skimpy blouses. It's even worse when you've got to roll down a flight of stairs."

Sonia was beginning to wonder why anyone would take this kind of punishment for a living. "What exactly is a car hit?" asked Sonia.

"You've seen it in the movies when the car hits somebody and they roll over the hood."

"I've probably seen it many times, but I've never thought about the stuntperson who is hired to actually get hit."

"It's not exactly like that," said Marlee with a laugh. "You'll see the way we do it."

On a wide flat area of dirt, Quinn was revving up the motor of an old Chevy. "You ever put any oil in this old heap?" he called to Dylan.

"Every couple of years. Why?"

Quinn howled with laughter. "This car's stayin' together out of sheer meanness."

"It may not look like much," Dylan told Sonia as they walked toward the rusty car, "but a body hitting a car can cause some pretty bad dents. This car's perfect for practice hits."

"A car can cause some pretty bad dents in people, too," she remarked with a shudder. "I can't believe you're actually going to walk in front of that car and let it hit you."

Dylan and Quinn both chuckled. "The trick is to make it look like it's hitting me, when actually I'm going to hit the car—first with my hands to break the impact, then roll over the hood on my shoulder."

He gave her a demonstration. As Quinn drove the car forward, Dylan took a few running steps and within seconds was rolling up over the hood and onto the ground. After standing up and brushing the dirt off, he came over to where she was standing. "See? Nothing to it."

Marlee made a pass at the car and Sonia was surprised that her hit was so much smoother than his, almost like a gymnastics move.

"Try that again," Dylan told her. "It looked too good."

"How can you be too good?" Sonia asked.

"Someone just bumped by a car doesn't float over it like a gazelle. A lot of stunt work is acting—in fact, we're even in the same union." Dylan told Marlee to slam her hands onto the hood to make a louder bang as she rolled over the car.

A few more and Marlee began to look considerably more injured. After each hit Sonia held her breath until Marlee stood up casually and brushed herself off calmly. Even from her close vantage point it seemed terrifyingly real.

Dylan began explaining Monday's stunt to Quinn.

"After the hit, I'm going to crouch down, then

start to run. You'll back up and come for me
again. There'll be some packing crates off to the
left. I'll jump up on them and you'll get out of the
car and come after me. We'll have about a
four-foot-square area to stage the hand-to-hand
fight."

"Four-feet?" Quinn groaned. "How the hell
can we do anything interesting for the camera in
a tight space like that?"

"We'll work it out."

As Sonia watched them pace out each move—
the angle he'd be running, the way the car would
catch him and where he'd fall—she began to
understand what Dylan meant when he said
everything was carefully planned out to mini-
mize danger. And yet, if they were a few seconds
off and the car made contact at the wrong angle,
Dylan could be killed. No wonder he desperately
needed all his faculties functioning clearly for
his work.

"This is strictly movie fighting," Marlee explained. "They have to exaggerate everything
for the camera. Dylan told me the first time he
and Quinn saw stuntmen go at it in a movie they
nearly laughed their heads off. I guess they'd
been in a few real knock-down, drag-outs in the
army. See how wide they're swinging, bringing
their arms way out? In a real fight you'd get
killed if you didn't keep your elbows real tight
into your body."

It wasn't long before the two men were sweat-
ing with exhaustion and covered head to toe
with dust. Quinn wiped his forehead with the

back of his hand. "I think we're ready for Monday. Time for a cold beer and a dunk in that pool."

Dylan readily agreed. "Did you remember to bring a bathing suit?" he asked Sonia.

"I know you mentioned it to me last night, but it slipped my mind."

"I'm sure I've got one that'll fit you," offered Marlee. "We're about the same size."

They might be about the same size, but the stuntwoman was much firmer in the places that counted. "That's really nice of you, Marlee, but I hate to borrow things."

"Don't be silly," she said quickly.

Marlee took her to a large bathroom with a door that opened out to the pool, and she opened a cabinet drawer. "There must be a half dozen bathing suits in here. You're welcome to any one you want."

"Which one are you going to wear?"

"Makes no difference to me. I like them all. You take one that appeals to you." She opened another drawer. "Sunscreen, extra makeup and stuff's in here, beach towels in the bottom drawer. I'll let you go ahead and change and I'll be back in a minute."

When she closed the door, Sonia let her face drop down with her spirits. If there was any question about Marlee's living there, this cleared it up. With half a dozen bathing suits in the bathroom, the whole wardrobe had to be in the bedroom closet.

In a way, it was a relief. She would have to put

those simmering kisses from last night out of her mind. Dylan was obviously only looking for a little extracurricular activity. Even his supposed precognition situated their lovemaking at her house, not his. If he was going to play around on Marlee, he planned to be discreet about it.

Sonia soon discovered that Marlee had daring taste in bathing suits, but then, the stuntwoman also had the body to squeeze into them. She set aside the skimpy bikinis in favor of a black, one-piece suit. Even though it was cut down to the navel in front and was equally daring in back and rode high on the hips, it was the most flattering to her figure.

When she went out to the pool, Quinn was already in the water, leaning up against the edge of the pool sipping a can of beer. "Come on in; it's great."

Dylan called out from the kitchen. "Sonia, would you like a beer?"

"I'd rather have a soft drink, if you've got it. Beer and sunshine put me to sleep."

When he came out with the drinks, Sonia drew in her breath at the sight of him. In swim trunks she got the full effect of his body—the long, muscled thighs and the hard, well-developed chest covered with dark hair tapering down to his abdomen. It occurred to her that it was the most magnificent body she'd ever seen. Every inch of him was honed for action.

Instead of a diving board at the deep end, there was a trampoline, and Sonia suspected he was showing off a little for her when he did a double somersault into the pool, slicing the water in perfect form.

Self-consciously she eased herself into the pool from the shallow end and sidestroked across to the other side.

"That was a beautiful dive," she said with admiration.

He shook his head free of water. "You ever done any diving?"

"The summer I was sixteen, my parents gave me lessons. They insisted it was a social necessity like tennis, but I hated getting up on a diving board. Something about looking down at the water from up there paralyzed me. The lifeguard finally gave up on the diving board and after six weeks settled for getting me off the side of the pool without a belly flop."

Marlee came out of the house in the skimpy red polka-dot bikini. Hers was another body finely tuned for action, with not an ounce of flab anywhere. Like Dylan, she made her pool entrance from the trampoline, doing an exquisitely graceful dive.

Shaking her blond hair back, she said, "Hey, guys, you want to try that backflip today?"

"Sure." Quinn put his beer down at the side of the pool, and Sonia watched as the two men crossed arms, gripping each other's wrists. Marlee deftly climbed up on them, resting her hands on the tops of their heads.

"Okay," said Dylan. "We'll go down, up, down; then we'll flip you over. Ready?"

She grinned. "Yup."

When the two men released her with a powerful thrust, Marlee flew up into the air, arching her back into the water. Her head popped back up in a minute. "That was fun. Let's do it again."

The men were happy to comply. When she came up the second time, Dylan said, "Hey, Sonia, you want to give it a try?"

"Yes, do," encouraged Marlee. "It's not really hard. You just relax and the motion does all the work for you."

"No, guys, I don't think so . . ."

In seconds, Dylan was beside her. "Come on, it's easier than you think."

"I'm the least coordinated person I know."

"You're not at all. Look how well you did on the tightrope."

"That was a fluke, and you were holding on to me. Doing a backflip when I can barely dive nose first would be impossible."

"You won't be going off a diving board," Dylan argued.

"Diving board, trampoline, wrists—what's the difference?"

"Try it, just once," he coaxed.

He and Quinn formed the bridge with their arms. "Put your hands on our shoulders and step up here."

Sonia backstroked away from them. "Thanks, but . . ."

"Come on." His voice was seductive.

"What if I break my neck?"

"You won't."

She thought about what Dylan had said about fear, and suddenly she wanted to prove that she had at least half as much guts as Marlee.

Their bodies were slippery as she stepped onto their crossed arms.

"Now stand up and put your hands on our heads."

She moved slowly from a crouching position, her knees wobbling. How had Marlee done this looking so graceful? Standing on their slippery wrists felt even less secure than the tightrope.

"We'll lower you down, up, down, then up and over," said Dylan. "Ready?"

She was still trying to retain her precarious balance on their arms. "No, wait a minute. Let's forget this whole thing. I'm chickening out."

"No you're not. You'll land in the water, so you won't hurt yourself. Now, ready?"

She gulped and nodded.

"Okay, relax," Dylan began. "Down, up, down and . . ."

Sonia didn't hear the last "up." Propelled by their powerful thrust, her body rocketed into the air. She felt her spinal cord twist backward in an arc so severe she thought it would snap; then a sudden cold rush of water enveloped her.

Frightened but unable to do anything, she decided not to fight against it and hoped the force of the motion would continue to propel her to the surface.

She badly needed air, but it seemed to have left her lungs. She had no sense of direction. Panic set in. Where was the surface?

McCabe's drowning-rat experiment flashed through her mind. How far do you go before you give up and die?

Suddenly she became annoyed with herself. She was supposed to be seeing her entire life flash before her eyes, and all she could conjure up was one of McCabe's rat experiments. She'd be damned if that would be her last memory on this earth!

She flailed her arms and opened her eyes. A partial sense of direction returned as she spied the surface of the pool. Cupping her hands, she pushed the water aside and put all her strength into swimming toward the light.

Seconds later she found herself gazing wide-eyed at Dylan.

"That was great for a first try!" he said. "Come on, do it again."

Could these people comprehend an absolute lack of physical courage? It might be shameful to admit such weakness, but she realized that if she was to live through the afternoon, she'd have to.

"No thanks, Dylan, that scared me witless. I think I'll sit this one out in the sun."

He followed her up the steps out of the pool. "Hey, you all right?" He slipped an arm around her waist, and amazingly, the steadying feel of it took away some of the shakiness.

She pushed the long, damp hair from her face. "I'm okay, thanks. But maybe I will have that beer now."

Marlee did some vigorous laps and was climbing out of the pool just as Dylan returned with more beer. "Did you happen to get a look at the clock when you were in there?" she asked him.

"It's about three-thirty."

"Yee gads," Marlee squealed. "I'm going to be late for my exercise class. See you guys later."

Sonia watched her run into the house to change. When Dylan settled into the chaise beside hers, she commented, "I can't believe Marlee's going to an exercise class."

"Why not?"

"She's done nothing but exercise all day!"

Dylan chuckled. "In this business there's no such thing as being too fit. Marlee works hard, and because of that she's one of the top stunt-women in the business."

Sonia quickly reminded herself that being in top physical condition could mean the split-second difference between life and death. "Is there a lot of prejudice against women in this kind of work?"

"You bet. Usually when a script calls for a woman, they stick a dress on a man. Nobody used to think a woman could handle the rough-and-tumble stuff. Women like Marlee are proving them wrong, but it's a constant uphill battle. The paychecks can be few and far between. That's why she's been trying to get into acting. It's a little more secure, and you've got some longevity. When a man gets too old to do stunts, he can at least move into stunt coordinating. But that field is even harder for a woman to break into."

Sonia had to admire Marlee for her tenacity

and independence. With the money Dylan made, she probably didn't have to work at all if she didn't want to.

"You don't attend any exercise classes?" he asked.

"Me? No." She laughed. "But don't tell anyone. I understand failure to attend an exercise class is a misdemeanor in Los Angeles."

He ran a hand down her arm. "But you have a beautiful body, good muscle tone. You must do something to keep it that way."

She smiled at the compliment. He was probably one of the few men who could talk about a woman's body as though it were a nicely constructed car engine.

"I jog about a half mile a day, don't consume many calories and lead a good clean life."

"That sounds dull. No men in your life?"

She adjusted her sunglasses. He was putting her on the spot again with those personal questions she'd been trained to avoid. And now that Marlee had left, he was probably leading her to the subject of an involvement with him.

She almost changed the subject, then reconsidered. It was human nature that one confession always brought on another. If you shared a secret, that implied an obligation to reciprocate.

Putting her personal feelings aside, she did want to help him over the nightmares. And perhaps if she loosened up and told him something of her life, he might open up about Marlee and eventually even discuss his childhood.

"I don't date much," she told him honestly.

"Why not?"

"It's always seemed to me rather pointless."

"I'd agree, but nobody's come up with anything better than these ancient courting rites for getting together with someone and falling in love."

"That's another reason I avoid it."

"You're not interested in an involvement?"

"Not at the moment," she hedged. "My schedule is too demanding. Relationships take time to build. I don't have that kind of time."

He brushed the back of his hand across her cheek. "You said last night that love eludes you. I'm beginning to think it's the other way around."

She took a long sip of the cool beer, then turned over on her stomach. "That's true, though I think some day I'd like to find the kind of relationship you have with Marlee." She congratulated herself on a superb lead-in and was surprised when he sat up and laughed.

"You think Marlee and I are going together?"

"You're not?"

"No. We're just good friends. Besides, she's been living with a hell of a nice guy for five years. They're going to be married in a few months."

"But the bathing suits . . ."

"She's been coming here to use the equipment for years and I've been helping her with stunts. It's just convenient to leave a couple of suits, leotards and jeans here. She even keeps a whole drawer full of makeup in the bathroom."

A weight lifted off Sonia's shoulders, but she regarded it with caution. Dylan might be free, but that didn't mean she could go running after him. It was like contemplating another backflip in the pool.

Quinn, who had been swimming laps, finally pulled himself out of the pool and plopped down on a chaise lounge nearby. Sonia was grateful for the break as the conversation drifted to the stunt they were going to do Monday.

When the sun's rays began slanting through the trees so that the pool was in shade, they all went inside to change. Since Quinn was leaving, Sonia thought it was best for her to say goodbye too.

Dylan rested a hand on her shoulder. "Stay awhile. I want to show you the photos from my circus days."

It was tempting. If he told her about the circus, maybe he'd be willing to go further back and talk about his reasons for leaving home.

Then again, if she stayed he might misinterpret it as meaning she wanted to stay and make love with him. And the problem was, deep inside she did.

Chapter 7

THE OUTSIDE OF DYLAN'S HOUSE MIGHT HAVE been sparsely landscaped, but the interior decor made up for it. On one long wall in the living room, over the big stone fireplace, was a weapons collection that included everything from Civil War rifles to African spears and Indian tomahawks.

His real pride, however, was in the circus posters. "Some of these are from the last century," he said proudly. "I'd been collecting them for years—I've got them from all over the world—but it wasn't until I bought the house and had a place to put them that I had them all framed."

In spite of the threatening weapons, Sonia liked the room. The floor was a dark polished hardwood with Oriental rugs, and the tan contemporary furniture had big fluffy cushions that one could sink into.

It would strike her later that the room expressed all the different aspects of Dylan's personality. The weapons showed the violence and adventure, in the circus posters were the excitement and drama, and the comfortable furniture reflected the warm, relaxed side of him that at first she didn't suspect.

He brought them each a glass of wine, then pulled out a large box from a closet and spread the pictures out on the coffee table.

"I keep meaning to have this stuff framed, or at least organize it in a scrapbook, but I never seem to get around to it. Did you ever keep a scrapbook when you were a kid?"

"Up until the time Jay Jay died. After that there wasn't much about my life I wanted to record for posterity. I don't even have pictures of myself from about ten to fifteen."

"Why not?"

"I used to throw them all away. I didn't like myself much."

"I don't have any pictures of myself before the circus, but that's because I didn't take anything with me when I left home."

She picked up a fuzzy dog-eared snapshot of a young boy with black hair and eyes mature beyond their years. "Is that you?" He was standing next to an elephant, a shovel in his hand.

"Elephant detail." He chuckled. "It was a good way to build up muscles."

A slightly older Dylan was in a glittering costume and standing on the back of a cantering white horse. Another showed him doing a somersault from one horse to another. He showed her a publicity photo of the entire equestrian troupe in similar costumes, white horses lined up in the background.

"The Colombo family," he said with affection. "They took me in and treated me like one of the family."

"Do you ever see them anymore?"

"When they're in L.A." He pointed to a little girl in the center. "Giuliana, this one, got married in Milan last summer and I flew over for the wedding."

He rummaged through some more snapshots. "This is when I started on the trapeze with the Gonzales family."

It was another group photo. Dylan stood taller than the others, his teenage body slightly gaunt. In spite of the smile, the eyes were intense.

He was proudest of the action photos of his trapeze work, and he explained each one in great detail.

"Flying was my great love," he said nostalgically. "Sometimes I wish I were still doing it."

"You could, of course."

He leaned back against the cushions. "No, you can't go back. It was like when I left home. I knew I'd never go back."

"There's no comparison with that. You still see your circus friends. Why did you run?" she asked softly.

He took a long sip of wine and looked out the window. The crickets were chirping loudly in the gathering dusk. It suddenly struck Sonia how lonely and isolated this house was. Having enough land to set up the circus apparatus probably was not his first consideration in buying it. He wanted to distance himself from others.

"My mother disappeared when I was about five," he began, then seemed reluctant to continue.

"She died?" Sonia prodded gently.

"I don't know. My dad would never talk about her and never let me mention her name. He used to beat her up pretty bad. For all I know he might have killed her. I . . . came home from school one day and she was gone. I'd like to think she got fed up and left, but then it would hurt to think she just up and left me there."

"Did you have any brothers and sisters?"

He shook his head. "And no relatives I knew about. My mother's family is still in Italy, I suppose, but I never knew her maiden name, so I have no way of checking."

"What finally made you decide to leave?"

"I used to fantasize about it a lot, but when you're a kid you don't have a lot of options. And we moved around so much, I didn't have friends to go to. I guess I was kind of lonely, so one day I brought home a dog, a crazy little mutt with his ribs showing. Somebody had just abandoned him in a park." He gazed up at the wall of weapons. "The old man came home and was ready to take me apart for having the dog. He kicked it, slammed it through a glass door. The dog was bleeding . . . I grabbed him and ran to a vet, but it was too late to do anything. So I just never went home again."

Dylan took a deep breath and let it out slowly. She knew instinctively that he'd never told anyone this before. Sonia closed her fingers around his hand.

"People ask me if I get scared doing stunts. Yeah, I'm scared, but the truth is, nothing—not even Vietnam—was as frightening as those years with my father."

"I've dealt with some child abuse cases. One of the worst things is being beaten by the very people you depend on for love and shelter."

"There was never any love," he said harshly. "One good thing that came out of it—I learned how to dodge swinging fists and how to make fast exits through bathroom windows, vault over fences and climb trees in the middle of the night. All that early training helped with acrobatics, and later with stunts. It's ironic that now I make a good living dodging fists and making spectacular escapes."

"It's not ironic at all. In fact, it makes perfect sense."

"How's that?"

"It's a way to relive your childhood."

"Why the hell would I want to do that?"

"Because this time you can be the one in control. You can even plan everything out ahead of time so you don't get hurt. It's a little like having the power to foretell the future." Another idea suddenly struck her. "When exactly did you first realize you were psychic?"

He dropped his head back against the couch and closed his eyes meditatively for a moment. "It wasn't anything specific—well, maybe little things like knowing what a teacher was going to ask on a test. But there was always a kind of sixth sense about when my father was going to come home boozed and knock me around. So I'd get prepared for it, like leaving windows open so I could escape fast if I needed to."

She turned to him excitedly. "Remember what I said to you about precognition? That it might be something we're all born with as a kind of survival tool? Most of us don't live in constant fear for our lives. Unlike cavemen, we don't need a sixth sense to tell us there's a leopard hiding up in the next tree ready to pounce on us. But when we are in danger or when a loved one is, that instinctive psychic mechanism can be activated."

"You mean I developed the precognition to protect myself against my old man?"

"You might have."

He paused in the stroking of her hand to pour her another glass of wine. In the growing darkness of the room, his eyes seemed almost black. "You psychologists go on the theory that everything we do is influenced by something that happened in our childhood, don't you?"

"That's an oversimplification. There are a lot of factors, but it's pretty much true."

He brushed his hand up under her thick dark hair and caressed her neck. "Did you ever consider that the reason you're afraid of going off a diving board into a pool is that you're remembering looking down into the water where your brother died?"

Her eyes widened. "I never thought of that."

He smiled and continued to caress the back of her neck, slowly removing the tension. "And something else occurs to me that goes with what you said this afternoon. You told me that the day your brother died you were running to see a boyfriend. I wonder if the reason you don't get involved with men is that you're afraid if you do, some great disaster will happen to you."

She nodded and sighed. "Now that is something a few shrinks have pointed out to me."

"You've been to psychologists?"

"And psychiatrists. Some of it was for my graduate training. You can't really give someone therapy if you don't know how it feels. Jay Jay was the light of my parents' life. They were from the old school where daughters didn't count for much; only sons mattered. In my mother's first hysterical burst of grief she even accused me of pushing him into the creek, of . . . trying to kill him."

There was the rush of adrenaline at the memory of her mother's accusations, the guilt over wondering if she wasn't at least indirectly responsible for Jay Jay's death because of her negligence. Dylan pulled her closer to him and the warmth of his body calmed her.

"You know how kids' imaginations are," she continued. "I thought they'd send me to the electric chair. In spite of the sibling rivalry, I really loved Jay Jay; but the guilt was burning me up. I stopped eating and refused to talk—to anyone. I was sure my parents hated me—that everyone in the world blamed me for my brother's death. Then a kind of fog set in and suddenly I found myself in an institution where all the kids were disturbed. A very talented and warm and wonderful psychiatrist finally brought me out of it."

"And that's why you decided to become a psychologist?" Dylan asked.

Without thinking about it, she rested her head on his chest. "I experienced firsthand how therapy could salvage a life."

He kissed the top of her head and rubbed his hand up and down her arm. "I guess neither one of us had a very ideal childhood."

"One thing I've learned in this work is that people are tremendously resilient. I've seen them come into the hospital so violent they had to be restrained in a straitjacket and kept in a padded cell, and then watched them recover, go home and lead normal lives."

He turned her face up to him. His gaze dropped briefly to her lips, then back to her eyes. It was the prelude to a kiss that she desperately wanted from him and yet knew she should avoid.

"Dylan, I think . . ."

His lips moved slowly, gently teasing her mouth open while his free hand swept seductively down her neck, grazing her breast and resting at the curve of her hip, igniting every nerve end along the way.

She started to pull away but he steadied her

head with his other hand. "Let it go, Sonia. It has to happen. I'm a fatalist; you and I were meant to come together."

"And then?"

He traced a thumb over her lips. "I can assure you nothing disastrous is going to happen."

"How much of the future have you seen regarding us?"

"I've seen us making love."

"Nothing beyond that?"

"It doesn't mean there won't be anything."

She sighed and wrapped her arms around his neck. "Then what good are you soothsayers anyway?"

"Darlin', you're about to find out."

Chapter 8

SONIA WANTED TO JUMP UP AND RUN FOR THE door or at the very least to say no, but desire for him outweighed every other concern. As his lips gently met hers, his hand slipped up over her rib cage and encircled a breast, his long fingers brushing the tip. Sonia drew in her breath as the sparks serpentined inside her.

Sensitive to her reaction, his mouth swept down across her cheek and neck. Deftly he unbuckled her belt and unzipped her jumpsuit. Pulling her up, he slipped it down over her arms. For a long moment he simply looked at her naked breasts, then into her eyes. "You're so beautiful," he whispered.

With slow deliberation he kissed each bare shoulder, then cupping a breast, he took the tip in his mouth, pulling and licking until it grew hard. Then he did the same with the other until the flames danced through her. All control slipping away, she sank back against the downy cushions and ran her fingers through his thick black hair, marveling at the silky texture.

His lips were on hers again, and this time the kiss was deep and passionate. He tossed some cushions to the floor and the couch suddenly became roomy as a bed. She was conscious of the strength of his body as it lengthened beside her.

His hand swept down from her neck and over her body. "I love the satin feel of you, Sonia. Ever since I first saw you I wondered how it would be to touch you. This afternoon I could barely keep my hands off you in that bathing suit."

Her breath was ragged. "I wanted you, too, but I've been afraid to admit it."

Gently he pulled the jumpsuit down over her legs until she was entirely naked, warmed only by the sultry gaze of his hooded turquoise eyes.

Watching her, he started to unbutton his shirt, but she beckoned to him. "Let me," she whispered.

Her fingers were trembling as she undid each button, revealing the strongly muscled chest she'd longed to touch when they'd sunbathed together by the pool. Combing her fingertips through the dark chest hair, she found his nipple and bent her head down to tease it with her tongue.

He raised her head up and covered her mouth

with his. Impatient to be free of his clothes, he didn't let her complete the task and flung them off himself. As their naked bodies pressed together, Sonia felt the shock of the smooth texture of his skin.

His hand slipped between her legs and caressed the insides of her thighs, his fingers moving tantalizingly close to the center of her desire. A moan escaped her lips as she felt his expert touch.

His long fingers rubbed and caressed until she was twisting, writhing with the exquisite agony. As with the backflip, she was being propelled by a more powerful force. Only this time she was not afraid.

"Yes, yes . . . please, Dylan," she begged huskily.

His first thrust was a gentle exploration that made the lower half of her body tremble. Then he grew bolder and all she could do was to wrap her legs around him and clutch tightly to his strong shoulders. They were on a careening roller coaster, racing and plunging, swerving dangerously, precariously out of control.

Just when she was sure she was at the height of her pleasure, Dylan changed his rhythm and increased the intensity again and again until an explosion burst in her depths, mushrooming through her body and followed by lightning spasms that continued long after he had stopped.

Later he held her in his strong arms and kissed the moisture on her forehead. She nuzzled her face into the hollow of his strong neck.

Never in her life had she felt so secure and happy, so . . . loved.

Hold it, Sonia, she cautioned herself. Making love wasn't the same thing as being loved. But whatever she'd found, it was too delightful to analyze for the moment.

He traced a finger across her lips and she bit it playfully.

"The tigress is hungry?"

"Maybe a little."

"I don't have much in the refrigerator. Want to go out, or shall I order us a pizza? We even have delivery service out here in the wilderness."

"With sausage and salami and olives—but no anchovies. I hate anchovies."

"We have that in common," he said with a laugh, and started to rise.

A pang of doubt suddenly seized her. "And not much else in common, I'm afraid, besides miserable childhood experiences."

He gathered her up in his arms and covered her face with kisses. "Sonia, my love, I wouldn't exactly call our relationship doomed because I don't do psychoanalysis and you don't do movie stunts."

She smiled slightly. "Maybe if I work on the tightrope . . ."

He ran his long fingers languidly over her body and smiled. "We've just discovered something wonderful we do have in common, besides an unreasoned hatred of anchovies. We'll survive."

He went into his bedroom and brought her out a thick blue terrycloth robe to keep warm, then telephoned for a large pizza. When it arrived,

Dylan insisted they go into the dining room and eat by candlelight.

In spite of the formal surroundings, they devoured the delicious pizza most inelegantly, that being "the only civilized way to handle pizza," according to Dylan.

"You've had no more dreams about the stunt you're doing with Marlee?" she asked as they ate.

"Not for a while. Maybe just knowing there's a way to end the dreams is a help."

"Then do you still want me to put you under hypnosis?"

"Maybe not." A piece of salami dropped onto his plate. He retrieved it and took a thoughtful bite. "I'd miss winning at the races. And precognition does come in handy for other things. What if I hadn't foreseen us making love? You might never have thought of it without my suggestion."

She lopped some dripping mozzarella back onto her slice of pizza and laughed. "Don't kid yourself. The first time you touched me, I felt a wonderful tingling."

"And now?"

She rubbed a bare foot up the calf of his leg. "Even more now."

After dinner they went back to his bedroom and cuddled under the covers. "Sonia, I meant it when I told you last night we had to be honest. I want you to know that I've never had feelings this strong for any woman before."

They were words she probably should have been relieved to hear, but for some reason Sonia felt herself pulling back. "Let's just take it slowly," she said cautiously.

"I've never taken anything slowly."

"This time you'll have to, Dylan. I told you how it is with my work. I talk to people about these things every day. Relationships require a lot of time. You have to care for someone and be responsible for them and . . ." She didn't know quite why, but tears clouded her eyes.

He smoothed her long hair out onto the pillow. In the semidarkness his eyes looked midnight blue.

"And that's like being responsible for a little brother," he finished for her.

She shut her eyes against his penetrating gaze. "Yes," she whispered.

He cradled her in his arms. "You don't have to think about it now. I won't rush you. But I'm not letting you go, either."

He swept a hand over her breasts and a surge of desire coursed through her. He felt it too, for she was suddenly aware of the growing hardness against her thigh. She reached down to caress him.

"Dylan, let's not talk about any of that tonight."

"You're right," he said huskily. "No more talk at all."

They made love again and fell into a deep sleep locked in each other's arms.

From the helicopter he could see the emerald jungle below, the scarlet smoke from the explosions.

"Go on down," Dylan said suddenly. "I see it."

"What do you see, man?" asked Quinn.

"The convertible, the red convertible."

"A red convertible here?"

They both laughed. It was funny to see a red convertible in the Mekong Delta.

Quinn lowered the helicopter, and as they got closer, Dylan's heart stopped. "Damn!"

"What's the matter, pal?"

"Marlee was supposed to be in the back seat of the car."

"Isn't she?"

"No, it's Sonia." A wave of fear gripped him. "What the hell is she doing there? She's not a stuntwoman."

"She was scared to do a simple backflip in the pool," Quinn agreed.

"I can't lift Sonia out of that car. She won't know how to grip. She's probably not even wearing wristbands."

Quinn shrugged. "What else can you do?"

"Get the director on the radio. Tell him I won't do the damn stunt unless he uses a regular stuntwoman. I want Sonia out of there."

Dylan's chest tightened as he watched the car below. He'd told Sonia never to be afraid and here he was putting her in danger. He couldn't let any harm come to her.

The director's voice over the radio had a familiar ring. The sound of it chilled him and raised beads of sweat that dripped down his chest.

"I'm not makin' no substitutes at the last
minute," the director screamed. "Tell that bastard the only way to get her out of there alive is
to rescue her like it says in the script."

"The man's crazy!" Dylan said.

The growling voice of the director blasted
through the speaker. "Tell Mario to go to hell. If
he wants her safe, he's gonna have to go down
there as planned and haul her out. Otherwise
I'm going to run her off a cliff."

Mario. With sinking recognition, he knew
now who it was. His father was directing this
movie; the one man he knew who was berserk
and mean enough to run her off a cliff.

Against Quinn's protests, Dylan started
down the ladder. A strong wind made the ladder swing back and forth, forcing him to de-
scend slowly. Attached to the bottom rung was
the trapeze bar. Sliding his legs through, he
motioned for Quinn to lower him down further.

He was close enough now to see Sonia's terrified expression and it pained him. God, how
he hated his father for putting her through
this.

He swung himself upside down and reached
toward her. "Sonia, honey, grab on to my
wrists. I'll pull you up."

"Dylan, I'm afraid. I don't know how."

"Clasp hard on to my wrists. I won't let you
go. Remember how I kept you on the tightrope.
Trust me; it's the only way out."

The driver speeded up so that he was suddenly left dangling over the rear end of the car.
"Slow down!" he yelled at the driver.

"The director wants it faster," the driver said, *indifferently.*

Quinn put him back in place just over Sonia. She reached her hands up tentatively. He touched the tips of her fingers ... so many things he had been able to see by touching the tips of her fingers, but now he saw only her frightened face. He had to get her out of there before the old bastard killed her.

Suddenly the helicopter dropped him down lower and to the right. He was alongside the car and dropping further. The pavement loomed up at him.

"Quinn, it's too far!" he shouted, though he knew Quinn couldn't hear him over the helicopter blades. "Pull me up!"

But he kept dropping down, his head nearly touching the spinning rear wheel.

Someone was screaming and Sonia was calling to him.

Then his head slammed into the pavement.

The bloodcurdling howl jolted her awake.

It was dark and she was in a strange bed, a man beside her. Panic gripped her throat and cut off her breath so she couldn't scream. Then the events of the night came back to her.

"Dylan?" She touched his arm gently.

He stirred in his sleep, rolled over and took her in his arms.

"Are you all right?" she asked.

"Hmmmm?"

He kissed her neck and his hands smoothed down over her naked body. All the sensations

he'd led her through during the night floated
back and enveloped her. She rested her hand on
his thigh and kissed the hollow of his throat.

"Dylan, you just screamed in your sleep."

His arms tightened around her. "I'm sorry I
woke you."

"Was it that stunt again?"

"Yes . . . only this time you were in it, and so
was my father . . ." He took a deep breath, then
let it out.

"Tell me about it."

He propped himself up on pillows and drew
her to him. Sonia rested her head on his broad
chest and ran her fingers lovingly through the
dark chest hair—a familiar terrain by now.

"It was so weird. Quinn and I were back in
Vietnam and laughing about a red convertible in
the Mekong Delta."

He rubbed his chin and smiled. "Strange how
things get so mixed up in dreams. We'll be on
location in the desert for that shoot, nowhere
near a jungle."

"What was I doing in the dream?"

"Instead of Marlee, they were using you as the
stuntwoman."

"Me?"

"I was furious because I knew you'd be
scared."

She shuddered at the thought, then sat up in
bed with a grin on her face. "Dylan, this is
wonderful!"

"Why?"

"Don't you see? This means we can rule out

precognition. There's not a chance in the world I'd do anything remotely resembling that stunt."

He looked relieved. "And there's no way my father would be directing. He was so drunk most of the time, he could barely keep a job in a gas station. Why do you suppose I saw him as a director?"

"He's the one in control, calling the shots, the one you have to answer to. And talking about him tonight put him on your mind."

"It's odd, but I haven't heard his voice in over twenty years, yet it still freaked me out."

"That's only natural. He had a terrifying power over you when you were too small to protect yourself. The fear of him was still buried in your subconscious. That's exactly the kind of thing that comes out in dreams. What happened to make you scream?"

"I almost had hold of you; then the helicopter dropped too low. I could see the rear wheel of the car and then my head hit the pavement."

"Is it feasible that could happen?"

"Not likely. Quinn's too good a pilot."

She nuzzled into the hollow of his shoulder. "Darling, I'm convinced that you're psychic—you've proven that in the lab. But I really don't think this is one of those instances."

"Then you're convinced this is just a case of good old honest fear?"

"Yes, but well-warranted fear. I wish I could talk you out of doing the stunt."

It suddenly occurred to her that the reason he might not be able to see beyond their making love was that he wouldn't be alive. Tears welled up in her eyes and caught in her throat.

"Can't someone else do the stunt, Dylan, and you can just concentrate on nice safe things like car hits and fistfights?"

He ran a soothing hand over her long, dark hair. "Before this afternoon you thought even that stuff was dangerous."

"Everything's relative," she said with a sigh. "That helicopter stunt makes a car hit sound like a tea party."

"I'm committed to do that stunt, Sonia. I can't walk out now. They're shooting in a couple of weeks."

"There must be another stuntman who could do it."

"There aren't many with circus experience who can pull off a trapeze stunt like that."

Sonia suddenly felt connected to the long line of women through the centuries who had tried to keep their men from running off to war. The strong presence of him, musky and warm with sleep, was tangible. He meant too much to her now. She couldn't lose him.

Sonia kissed the beard-roughened cheeks, the smooth spirals of his ear, the crinkles at the corners of his eyes. His large, strong hands swept down over her, bringing back all the sparks of passion that had been theirs earlier that night.

He raised her up so that his lips could surround the tip of her breast, and his tongue flicked back and forth. His hand slid down to encircle her hips, then pressed between her legs, his long fingers doing magical, wondrous things that made her twist and moan.

His own breathing grew ragged as his mouth closed on hers, demanding with the raging needs flaming through them.

She stroked him in return and, craving the culmination of their love, tried to pull his hand away, but he wouldn't let her. "Not yet," he said in a low voice.

His mouth moved down from her breasts to her rib cage and lingered at her navel. He was pushing her legs apart, fingernails grazing lightly on the soft insides of her thighs. He was nipping there, gentle bites and licks and gusts of breath, moving closer with each agonizingly long minute to the center of her passion. The lower half of her body was wracked with tremors as he orchestrated the crescendos again and again. Then he moved up beside her and stroked her hair.

Sonia kissed him softly and guided him to her. "Oh, Dylan . . . ," she whispered as he filled her. She looked up with wonder at the luminous eyes framed in black gazing down at her. He folded her knees up and thrust again, this time deeper. After pulling out slowly, ever so slowly, he drove in again and whispered her name.

She was moaning, clutching at his hard hips, pulling him into her soul. Her eyes closed; she felt part of him with the culmination of their desire.

When they were lying quietly again in each other's arms, he said, "I feel better about the dreams now. I don't think I'll have them again. Let's forget about the hypnosis."

"As long as you realize it's your awareness of the real dangers involved that is bringing on those nightmares. I still wish you'd consider dropping it."

"Where would you draw the line next time? If I'd told you I was going to ski off a cliff, you would have told me not to do that either."

She hugged him tighter. It was futile. "Have you ever thought about taking up accounting?"

"Never."

"Plumbing?"

"No."

"How about science? You said you had an aptitude for it, remember?"

He laughed.

"A psychologist is not without resources. Let me try another approach." She cleared her throat and began in her most professional tone, "Did it ever occur to you that your wanting to do dangerous stunts has a lot to do with your need to be loved and accepted?"

"What sort of Freudian freeway brought you to that conclusion?"

As she smoothed her fingers over his cheek, he turned his head and kissed the palm of her hand.

"Well, when you first left home and joined the circus, risking your neck with equestrian acrobatics was the quickest way to become part of a family. Once you showed yourself capable and gutsy, the Colombos took you in. So you associate doing crazy stunts with acceptance and love."

"So if you accept and love me as a desk clerk, I won't feel the need to perform stunts anymore?"

She smiled and traced a finger across his sculptured lips. "See how quickly you catch on? Now that you understand what's behind it, you can take a course in bookkeeping and we'll both be happy."

He nipped at her finger. "You're forgetting one important factor."

"What's that?"

"I also enjoy what I do."

"You'll get over that."

"If McCabe told you that you had to stop psychical research to devote your energy to running rats through mazes, how would you feel?"

She rested her head on his hard chest. "You have the most annoying way of turning things back on me."

He gave her bottom a playful swat. "I can see I'll have to keep you in line. Now let's try to get some sleep. Tomorrow morning, what do you say we take a drive out to Malibu for a champagne brunch?"

"You come up with wonderful ideas."

"I've got a million of them where you're concerned."

"Oh? Tell me."

"We'd be up all night."

"Just the first few hundred or so."

"Go to sleep darlin'. With any luck we'll dream about them."

Chapter 9

THEY SLEPT TOO LATE ON SUNDAY MORNING TO make it to Malibu in time for brunch and decided instead on a late lunch. Since Sonia needed to change, Dylan followed her in the Cobra.

As they walked through her front door, he looked around in amazement. Although she had painted the walls a light, neutral gray with matching gray carpets and drapes, almost everything else in the room glowed with bright colors. "So this is the real Sonia Barnes."

"Don't let it out," she joked. "I have an image to protect."

On the roomy red couch were throw pillows in every imaginable color, while on the walls huge abstract paintings reflected the color scheme. He sat her down on the couch and stood back. In her scarlet jumpsuit and green belt, she blended into the colorful decor. "You're like one of those exotic, tropical flowers."

"My mother is Romanian, and I've always suspected a touch of gypsy in the family tree, though she'd never admit it."

"A gypsy, yes, that's what you are. I knew a gypsy once in the circus, and you remind me a little of her."

"Was that . . ." She was almost afraid to ask, then decided to plunge ahead. "Was that the woman you were in love with?"

"No, but Zenobia was a wonderful person, a fortune-teller complete with bandana and crystal ball."

"Was she psychic?"

"No, Zenobia was a phony, but an honest phony. She didn't try to put anybody on in the circus; it was just a way to make money. She used to tell people there would be romance or money coming into their lives. But she knew enough about actual fortune-telling to see that I did have talent. She's the one who taught me about using fingertips. I did that with her one day and predicted a tall, dark and handsome stranger who would sweep her off her feet. She nearly kicked me out of the trailer for that. Then a couple of weeks later a dark, handsome stranger came to have his fortune told—and Zenobia, for the first time in her life, saw the future clearly in that crystal ball. She married him and now they have a successful hardware store in Grand Rapids."

"It must be nice to have a tall, dark, handsome man come into your life and sweep you off your feet," she mused lazily.

"Wilder things have happened." He laughed and lifted her off the couch.

"Good grief, it's happening!"

She wrapped her arms around his neck as he carried her into the bedroom and lowered her gently onto the bed.

"I think I like being swept off my feet by tall, dark, handsome strangers," she whispered as he planted featherlight kisses over her face.

Suddenly he rolled onto his back and looked around. "So this is the bedroom."

"Is it what you saw that day in my office?"

"Pretty much. You do like bright colors, don't you?"

"Mmmmm."

He pulled her onto him and gathered her long hair up in his hands as he gazed into her eyes. "Dr. Barnes, there's a wild, uninhibited side of you I bet most people would never suspect. And you know what?"

"What?" She nibbled on his lower lip and moved sensuously on him.

"I like it." His kiss was deep and full of wild, hungry passion. She drifted into the delicious sensations, eager to satiate herself with them, when suddenly the doorbell rang.

She started to answer it, but he drew her back down.

"Ignore them and they'll go away," he suggested.

It was tempting. Looking into those black-fringed turquoise eyes, she wondered how she could ever consider leaving him, even for a moment.

The doorbell rang again. "If it's somebody who knows me, they'll see my car out front, and if I don't answer they might think something's terribly wrong and get the police or the paramedics to break down the door."

He laughed and let her up. "And I thought I had an imagination."

The doorbell rang again with angry insistence.

She smoothed her hair, zipped up her jumpsuit to a respectable height and smiled at him. "Wait right here and I'll tell whoever it is to get lost."

"How hospitable."

She stole a backward glance at him. "Did anyone ever tell you that you look delectable on a red bedspread?"

"I'd look even more delectable under it." He stood up and pulled it down. "Go get the door."

Whoever was there was impatient for her attention and rang again.

Generally she would have asked who it was before answering, but this time she was too preoccupied with the thought of Dylan in her bed and simply opened the door.

Walt Anguin rushed in, flushed and excited. "Dr. Barnes, I'm so glad you're home. I've been trying to call you all morning!"

Sonia could barely hide her irritation at seeing him. There were a few direct questions she

wanted to put to him. Why hadn't he called Dr.
McCabe to cancel her appointment? Why had
McCabe suddenly been inspired to visit the lab?
And what had Walt been doing in the hospital
parking lot Friday night when he was supposed
to be home sick with the flu?

But the answers to those questions might take
more time and effort than she wanted to give
him right now. Sunday was her day off, and with
Dylan Hamlin in the next room, the last thing
she wanted to deal with was Walt Anguin.

"Is it really important?" she asked coolly. "I'm
rather busy."

He was too keyed up to notice her icy recep-
tion. "I just had to show you these." He thrust
some photographs into her hands. "I was at the
lab last night doing Kirlian photography. You
know how we've been trying to duplicate the
experiment of the phantom leaf? Well"—he
gulped excitedly—"I did it!"

All at once Sonia forgot her anger and eagerly
went through the photos. What she saw set her
heart pounding. "Walt, this is phenomenal." She
was so thrilled she nearly hugged him, then
thought better of it. "We've been trying to get
that for over a year! I was beginning to despair it
could ever be done."

Dylan's voice broke in. "What in the world is a
phantom leaf?"

Walt's jaw dropped as he saw Dylan standing
in the bedroom doorway.

In the initial excitement Sonia had nearly
forgotten about him. She should have known he

would not take kindly to being ignored, but she wished he'd stayed hidden until Walt left.

To cover up the embarrassment of his making an entrance from the bedroom, she quickly explained what the photos meant. "You remember the Kirlian photography we were doing the other afternoon?"

His lips twisted into a half smile. She knew he was thinking about the kiss. "How could I forget?"

Walt looked away furtively. Guilt, thought Sonia. He must have been spying on them that afternoon.

Pushing her annoyance aside, she hurried on with her explanation. "The Russian couple who invented this photography shot a picture of a fresh leaf and discovered that plants have auras just like people. Then they snipped off a piece of the leaf and took another picture. It was the strangest thing. You could see a cut mark, but the missing part of the leaf still showed up—fainter, but definitely still there. Like a phantom. Walt and I have been trying to duplicate that experiment but to no avail—and now he's managed to do it."

Dylan examined the photos. "This is before the cut and this one's after," Walt said proudly.

"What's it mean?" asked Dylan.

"Nobody's certain, but some psychics have said that they can look at an amputee and still see the missing limb in a kind of aura."

"I remember in Vietnam when a buddy of mine lost his arm, he kept saying he still felt it was there sometimes. Do you suppose it has anything to do with that?"

"Possibly. I was beginning to believe the Kirlian experiment had been faked, but here it is! How did you manage to do it, Walt?"

"It would be hard to explain without getting into the watts and volts of the matter. But I was thinking of a way we could duplicate it with animals."

Sonia stiffened. "How, exactly?"

"Why don't we ask McCabe for some of his rats; then we could amputate part of their tails and—"

"Good God, Walt! That's so morbid. McCabe does enough awful things to those poor creatures in the name of science. I'll have no part of it. I feel bad enough about mutilating a leaf."

Walt looked as though he'd been slapped in the face and took a belligerent, defensive stance. "Did you ever stop to consider how many vaccines would never have been invented if animals hadn't been used? What about pacemakers?"

"All right," she conceded reluctantly, "but those things were to help people. What we're doing doesn't have any application to the public good." Sonia felt her cheeks grow hot. "Walt, just forget it. We'll do some more experiments with leaves, but nothing, absolutely nothing, with animals."

He wasn't ready to give up. "We don't know what any of this means. It might have some human application we haven't even thought of. Some of the greatest scientific contributions of all time have been accidental discoveries." He turned to Dylan for a potential ally. "You're not sentimental about rats, are you?"

"Not in the least. As a kid, I used to wake up in the middle of the night and find them nibbling on my toes. But I respect Sonia's convictions."

Walt curled his thin upper lip sullenly and glared alternately at him and then Sonia. "I can do experiments on my own, you know. McCabe would let me."

"I'm sure he would," she said tightly. It was an effort to keep the lid on her seething anger.

"Look, if it hadn't been for me, you wouldn't even have had any Kirlian photography," he snapped. "I'm the one who figured out how to put that contraption together from the Russian diagrams."

Sonia made an effort to keep her voice steady. "Walt, I'm very grateful to you. But this is one area that is off limits. I have never in my life done an experiment that put any living creature in pain, and I'm not about to begin now."

Walt's pale skin flushed scarlet. "I don't think you appreciate me in the least. You've never considered me anything more than a glorified janitor. In all this time I've known you, you've never asked me to call you Sonia instead of Dr. Barnes. Any time I've ever suggested we go out to dinner, you've turned me down. I've been loyal to you, done all your dirty work, and you still treat me like I'm beneath you. Then this slimy stuntman walks in one day out of the blue and you jump into bed with him."

Remembering the way Dylan could fight, she

could only pray Walt was thinking clearly
enough to realize he was no match for a man
who staged barroom brawls for a living. And she
didn't know Dylan well enough to know if he'd
go after someone over an insult. She flashed a
look at him. For the moment, anyway, he appeared alert and watching.

"Walt," she said carefully, "I think we should
discuss all this on Monday when you've had a
chance to cool off. Obviously there are some
problems I wasn't aware of, and we need to get
them out in the open."

"What's the matter with right now? Or do you
want to get back into bed with that stinking . . ."

Dylan pinned Walt with his eyes. "Walt," he
said quietly without moving, "I think you'd better leave."

Walt backed off a few steps. "I'm going to tell
Dr. McCabe you threatened me."

"Nobody threatened you," Sonia answered,
assuming the professional calm she used to
quiet her disturbed patients. "I just think it's
better if we discuss this rationally tomorrow at
work."

"I don't see where there's anything more to
discuss," he snapped, and slammed the door
behind him.

Sonia took a deep breath and exchanged a
glance with Dylan. "He left his precious photos," Dylan said, placing them on the coffee
table.

She sank down on the couch. "The really
awful part about all this is that Walt's right

about my attitude toward him. I never saw him as much more than a servant. He was just so self-effacing and efficient and willing to do anything for me that I took him for granted. I never wanted to let him get on a first-name basis because calling me Dr. Barnes kept a certain distance between us." She sighed wearily. "This is how the British must have felt when the empire began to break up and all their former colonies declared war on them."

Dylan joined her on the couch. "What's really bugging Walt is not the master-servant relationship. He's in love with you and probably would have gone on happily worshiping his goddess from afar. But when I stepped into the picture, it suddenly proved you were accessible—just not to him and it's driving him crazy."

Sonia gazed absently at the photos, then picked one up with renewed interest. "Walt has a brilliant mind. I just wish he could channel it in the right direction. Away from me."

Dylan took the photo from her hand and slipped an arm around her. "Now, where were we when we were so rudely interrupted?"

As he kissed her, she thought about all the years she'd used her job as an excuse to avoid becoming involved with anyone. Maybe it was because no man had ever intrigued her as much as her work. When she was in Dylan's arms, nothing else seemed to matter.

It was dinnertime before they arrived at the Malibu restaurant, which was famous for its seafood. Dylan made certain they had a table overlooking the ocean. She was happy, sparkling and bubbling like a Kirlian photograph or a bottle of champagne. After dinner, as they sipped Armagnac, Dylan reached across the candlelit table to take her hand and lifted it to his lips.

"I'm worried about Walt," he said suddenly.

"Another premonition?"

"Maybe—and what I saw this morning. Can he really do experiments without you?"

"Sure. If he came up with something McCabe and the board thought was worth funding, they'd go along."

"And this business with the rat tails, does that stand a chance?"

Sonia smiled. "You should have seen the fight I had to get any funds for parapsychology. But then again, if it had something to do with rats, McCabe might take more of an interest. He read about an experiment where they were trying to determine if rats had precognition. The researchers had a rat colony, and every day they'd pick a rat out randomly and kill it in front of the others. They were hoping to see if the rats would eventually develop a sense of who would be next."

"It sounds like something a demented Nazi in World War Two dreamed up."

"It's the way a lot of these researchers operate," she said with a sigh. "Anyway, it's the only parapsychology experiment I ever saw McCabe enthusiastic about. He suggested I try the same sort of thing."

"What did you tell him?"

"That I didn't see any point in finding precognition in rats. It was only humans who interested me, and I thought the university might not take kindly to our doing that sort of experiment with people."

Touching the tips of her fingers lightly, he closed his eyes for a minute.

She suddenly realized that he was trying to pick up on her future. "Dylan!"

He opened his eyes and looked at her a long minute.

"I don't want you to do that," she protested.

"Why not, if it can help you?"

"I just . . . I don't know. It makes me uncomfortable. And besides, before you knew me or Walt it was okay, but now that you're wrapped up in the middle of it, too many factors are working. Your imagination and feelings for me could get muddled up in it, and I'll start expecting things to happen that won't."

He laced his fingers through hers. "So you don't want to know what I just saw?"

She slanted a flirtatious gaze up at him. "It depends. I've become rather attached to one of your premonitions."

He laughed softly. "Well, to tell you the truth, I didn't see anything to do with Walt just then."

"What did you see?"

"It might have been my imagination, but it was superb." He gave her a mischievous wink. "We'll find out tonight if it meant anything."

* * *

Sonia was feeling a little giddy during her nine o'clock lecture Monday morning. At odd moments Dylan would pop into her mind and her body would do strange things. At the most improper moments, she found herself trying to suppress a silly smile.

Textbook symptoms of love?

Possibly. As a psychologist she knew this present euphoria could be an illusion. And if you weren't a rat with an electrode implanted in your brain and a lever to push for gratification, pleasure could be a transitory state.

Dylan was more volatile and exciting than any man she'd ever met, and although those qualities guaranteed an exciting romance, they didn't always get you through the long rocky haul of a relationship. A man who blithely risked his life for a living risked nothing by making love to a woman who was willing. Caught up in the flaming attraction, she had given herself to him after barely knowing him. How could she be sure it really meant anything to him? Sexual freedom and new morality aside, making love still made a woman vulnerable to being hurt. What if he never called again?

It was disgusting that after all those years of liberation it still came down to whether or not he called again. There were women who wouldn't hesitate to call a man, but Sonia didn't have the nerve for it. Independent as she was in other matters, she would still wait for him to make the next move.

Of course she would see him again for the experiments in precognition. Whatever else he might be, he was a man who kept his word in his business commitments. He was determined to do that dangerous stunt because he had given his word on it.

So then why should she doubt what he had to say about his feelings for her? Was she still, as a psychologist had once suggested, feeling like a little girl rejected by her parents, unworthy of love? Was she still terrified the sky would cave in if she ran after love?

After class she hurried to her meeting with McCabe. It wouldn't do to be late after that embarrassing scene Friday night. She wondered if it were possible to face a meeting with Rat McCabe without the same churning stomach she felt before a dentist appointment. Today would be a drilling without benefit of novocaine.

McCabe's secretary squinted up at her from her typing. "Dr. McCabe is tied up at the moment. He told me to ask you to wait."

"Thanks." She took a chair near the secretary and glanced at a women's magazine featuring an article by one of her colleagues. Sometimes it seemed every other psychologist was writing a book on sex and appearing in magazines and on TV talk shows. She mused that, after two nights with Dylan, she could probably write her own lengthy volume on the subject. Maybe two.

After twenty minutes of waiting, Sonia began

to be annoyed. She had made an effort to be on time, so why couldn't McCabe show her the same courtesy?

The door to his office finally opened. Her stomach actually felt queasy when she saw who walked out.

Walt shot her a malicious smirk, but said nothing.

Chapter 10

"Come in, Dr. Barnes, and have a seat." McCabe's voice was coolly gracious. "We have a good many things to discuss. Close the door, will you please?"

Since McCabe didn't do therapy he had no need for comfortable furniture. Sonia wondered if he had only ordered these stiff, backbreaking chairs to keep people uneasy in his presence.

He sat back in a chair that squeaked and lit a cigarette, inhaling and blowing the smoke out through his nose.

"Dr. Barnes," he began, then cleared his throat. "You know that we have never seen eye to eye on this parapsychology nonsense."

"I wouldn't call it nonsense." It might be unwise to goad him, but it was important to establish an early defense. If she were to concede these first minor skirmishes, she'd be backed against the wall when he launched the major assault.

Ignoring her protest, he steamrollered ahead. "The research you're doing is a joke. It's made this hospital the laughingstock of the academic community here."

"We have also merited high praise from a number of reputable psychiatric institutions for my work. I had more publications last year than any other psychologist on staff."

He took a short, irritated drag on his cigarette and spoke through the smoke. "Parapsychology is too far out of the mainstream, and the results of these experiments don't benefit anyone."

She wanted to ask if his rat research benefited anyone either, until the old adage about discretion being the better part of valor sealed her lips. She would take a pragmatic tack, hoping it would be more appealing. "ESP and precognition could have serious application by the military."

"Then let the military pursue it."

"I have reason to believe they already are. Now if we could—"

He drowned out her words by raising his voice. "Then I shall write to my congressman about the waste of taxpayers' money. Come on, Dr. Barnes. You're playing parlor games. Nobody's ever going to be able to mind-read."

"A few decades ago nobody ever thought you could transmit the sound of the human voice across miles and miles either."

"The results of your experiments so far have

been inconclusive; the responses you call ESP are pure coincidence."

"That's not true. We've shown ESP exists; now we're trying to figure out how people develop and transmit it. I've just found a subject who has strong evidence of precognition, and he's able to perform in a laboratory environment. Just imagine the application if people could learn how to see into the future."

"If you could see into the future, Dr. Barnes, you would see that your funds are about to run out," he said curtly. "You're wasting our time, our lab space and our money. From what I hear, you're running off to the races, using university funds for pari-mutuel tickets . . ."

"Dr. McCabe . . ."

". . . wasting film on pictures of leaves and finger pads, getting romantically involved with your patients."

"Dr. McCabe." She pounded his desk with her fist to get his attention. "If you're referring to Dylan Hamlin, he is not a patient of mine."

"He didn't come to you for some hypnotherapy?"

She flushed. "Well yes, originally, but then he decided not to go through with it and he's been participating in some of our experiments."

"I caught a glimpse of one of those experiments the other night." McCabe leaned forward menacingly. "Getting involved with a laboratory subject is not quite as bad as seducing a patient, but it's still highly unorthodox and unprofessional."

There wasn't much she could say to that, but

she could defend herself on the horse races. "The day we went to San Felipe, we were investigating Dylan's claim that he could predict winners."

McCabe rolled his eyes. "I heard all about that day at the races."

"He insisted on betting his own money. Walt and I bet two dollars each race for a total of thirty-six dollars. I have the pari-mutuel ticket stubs in my file. I'll show them to you."

"I have them right here, Dr. Barnes." He opened a file and showed her. "Your assistant brought them to me this morning."

"Then you can see for yourself," she said with relief.

He took a handful of tickets. "There is more than two hundred dollars' worth here. How do you explain that?"

Sonia's mouth fell open. "I . . . I don't know. Unless . . ." Suddenly she remembered that Walt had been placing bets on some of Dylan's choices, the ones that hadn't panned out. "Walt was making some extra bets," said Sonia. "Those may be his ticket stubs or he might have picked them up off the ground."

"Are you implying that Walt Anguin lied to me? That is a serious accusation."

Sonia sat up very straight and leveled her gaze at him. "I can only tell you that *I* am not lying to you. And I'm sure Mr. Hamlin would verify what I have to say."

"I'm sure he would," McCabe said sarcastically. "Dr. Barnes, you have flagrantly abused the privilege of your position here, and muddied the reputation of a fine, distinguished academic institution. Your status as professor and therapist will be evaluated separately, but as of now, you are not to conduct any more experiments."

She had to give it one last desperate stab. "Please, Dr. McCabe, just let me tell you about the experiment I'm conducting tomorrow." When he didn't object, she pulled out all the stops, telling him how Dylan had been able to pick up on her little brother's drowning. She detailed the results of the experiments she'd done with him so far.

McCabe looked bored, but at least he wasn't stopping her, so she continued to describe what she knew of Dylan's childhood and how he might have come by his unique psychic abilities. "Some studies have already indicated that actors have a higher incidence of ESP than the general population, and I think the same might be true of stuntpeople."

McCabe leaned back in his chair. "Why do you suppose that is?"

Clutching on to this thread of reluctant interest, she plunged ahead enthusiastically. "Stuntpeople are basically actors. If the script calls for a fall off a building, they don't just drop off and float down into an air bag, they flail their arms and legs to make it look as though they're really in trouble. They take a few words on a script and have to visualize what the writer meant and translate it into meaningful action."

"That sounds to me like an example of the creative process," said McCabe.

"I think the creative process involves a lot of

ESP. If you'll let me go through with the experiment tomorrow, at least I can establish if Dylan Hamlin has a higher incidence of ESP and precognition when it involves stunts he's actually done."

"What sort of controls have you set up?"

"Two more stuntpeople will see the exact same videotapes so I can compare their responses. What I'd really like to do is build up a lot of statistics with stuntpeople for comparison."

McCabe frowned. "All right, Dr. Barnes. Go ahead with the experiment tomorrow."

"And if tomorrow's results are significant?"

He stubbed out his cigarette in an overflowing ashtray. "After you complete your experiment tomorrow, your lab will be dismantled."

"But . . ."

"It's over, Dr. Barnes. I'm sick and tired of this foolishness. You want precognition? I'll give you precognition. You're not going to get any significant results tomorrow. I'm just letting you do this to complete your study, then I don't ever want to hear a word about parapsychology again."

As she walked back down the hall to her office, her shoulders slumped in exhaustion. It had not been a total defeat, but it wasn't much of a victory either, and there were still the accusations of misconduct. Walt's lies infuriated her. Funny how nobody ever said "Hell hath no fury like a *man* scorned." And it was his word against hers. If McCabe wouldn't accept Dylan's testimony, there was no way to clear her name.

The possibility of actually getting fired from her job was something she'd never considered before. Where would she go? Getting fired from a major university for misconduct and misappropriation of funds was not much of a recommendation.

When she returned to her office, she found Walt sitting there unable to meet her gaze. "I changed my mind," he said softly. "I want to talk."

"Good. But let's get out of here and take a walk in Student Park."

It was proving to be a scorcher of a day, but along the tree-lined paths it was cool. Walt hung his head and kicked at pebbles. "I guess I really messed things up."

"That's an understatement. All this because you couldn't call me by my first name?"

"Well, it had to do with the rats and . . ."

"Dylan Hamlin?"

"Yeah, that too."

She broke off a geranium leaf and studied it. "How come we never tried a geranium leaf?"

He shrugged. "I don't know. We tried just about every other kind."

"Well, it's a moot point now," she said sadly.

Walt's thin lips turned down. "And just when I finally got the phantom leaf."

She tossed the geranium leaf into a bush. "He's letting me continue with the precognition experiment tomorrow, but after that, he's dismantling the lab totally."

Walt looked crestfallen. "I really screwed up. I figured if I told McCabe that you'd been abusing funds, he'd let me do the rat tail experiment, but he was just pumping me all along for ammunition to get rid of you."

"He didn't like your rat experiment idea, I take it."

"No, and he thought I'd faked the phantom leaf. He said the whole thing was an embarrassment to the university." He shoved his hands in his pockets. "Wow, this whole thing sure backfired. Did me no good at all."

"Nor me," she added pointedly.

"Yeah. Look, I'm sorry. I'd really like to help you with that experiment tomorrow. It would help make up for some of what I did. I feel so lousy, I'd do anything to make it up to you."

They walked in silence for a few minutes. On the one hand, she no longer trusted Walt; but on the other, Walt knew the equipment and could conduct these experiments blindfolded.

"On one condition," she said.

"Anything."

"That you tell McCabe the truth about those pari-mutuel tickets."

"If I do that, he'll think I lied to him in the first place," he whined.

"Which you did!"

"But he was planning to cut off parapsychology anyway, so I don't see where this makes any difference now. Look at it from my point of view. I'm working on my master's degree. I could do myself a lot of harm by admitting I misrepresented the facts."

"Misrepresented the facts? That was a malicious, bald-faced lie!"

"I don't see where this is such a big deal. After all I've done for you these last two years, it's the least you could do for me."

"Go to hell," she said quietly, and turned on her heel.

Sonia spent most of the afternoon in the television department choosing stunt scenes from Dylan's and Marlee's tapes and transferring them to her own videocassettes. She also found another assistant, a young woman tape editor, who volunteered to help run the equipment for the experiment.

Sonia checked back at her office for a message from Dylan, but there was none in her box. And there was none on her service when she got home.

He had said he was going on location to the desert. There were all kinds of deserts in Southern California. That could have been anywhere. Palm Springs? Mohave? Palmdale?

She started to change into her jogging clothes, then thought better of it. What if he called when she was out and she missed the call? Well, what if he did! She couldn't spend every second glued to her telephone.

While jogging, she tried to put him out of her mind. Impossible. As long as he persisted in occupying her thoughts, she tried to concentrate on details of their lovemaking instead of car hits and the rough way he and Quinn had tumbled and tossed each other around.

By the time Sonia got back from her run, the sun was going down. How long could they shoot,

anyway? Surely they wouldn't continue after
dark.

It was futile to worry about him. He did this
kind of thing for a living, she told herself over
and over again. He and Quinn had rehearsed
every move.

What if he were home already and he simply
hadn't called? He could have been home hours
ago and already be out with another woman.

Of course, she had a perfect excuse to call
him. He was scheduled to be in the lab tomorrow
for the experiment. She could say she was calling just to reconfirm. But Dylan would know.

She glared at the telephone and opened her
textbooks. There was a lecture to prepare for
Wednesday, but the type on the page blurred as
she tried to read, and Dylan's face kept coming
back to her.

Wishing she'd jogged farther and worn herself
out, she paced the room and jogged in place. For
the first time in her life she longed for a television set. Even the canned laughter of a situation
comedy would be better company than this
empty silence filled with anxiety.

When he still hadn't called by midnight, she
fixed herself some herb tea and climbed into
bed. It had been wonderful there the night before with Dylan. She had slept peacefully in his
strong arms, and the few times she'd awakened
and stirred, he had wrapped himself more se-
curely around her and kissed her gently.

That he hadn't had a nightmare only recon-
firmed her conviction that it had been a combi-

nation of suppressed memories and fear about the helicopter stunt.

The next morning, bedraggled and bleary-eyed, she pulled herself together with an extra cup of coffee and dragged herself to work. She had slept only fitfully, tossing and tangling her legs in the sheets, wondering why he hadn't called.

The new assistant was already in the lab, excited to get started. Since the young woman had long since mastered the more sophisticated equipment in the television department, setting up the microphone and running the department's videocassette recorder was a snap.

Everyone was scheduled to arrive at ten o'clock, and as the hour approached, Sonia grew nervous. When the door to the lab opened she jumped. It was Quinn, Marlee and another stuntman friend of theirs, whom Quinn introduced as Randy.

"Dylan's not with you?" Her voice was shaky. All of the horrible things she'd imagined the night before ran through her mind.

"You mean he's not here yet?" asked Marlee.

"No." She tried not to betray the turmoil seething inside her.

"We were late on the shoot," said Quinn casually. "Maybe he overslept."

"Dylan Hamlin?" Marlee scoffed. "When have you ever known him to oversleep?"

Quinn shrugged. "Yeah, I guess you're right. He's got this inner clock. Tell him to wake up at six A.M. and he doesn't even need to set an alarm. Only time it didn't work was when we were in the army and making time changes."

As he was talking, Sonia suddenly noticed he was wearing a cast on his right arm. "What happened to your arm, Quinn?"

"Nothing serious. Dylan and I were doing that fight scene you saw us practicing. The platform was even smaller than the area we'd used to rehearse. I took a step backward, fell and busted my wrist." He shrugged. "In this business it happens all the time. I've probably busted every bone in my body at one time or other."

"Does that mean you won't be able to fly the helicopter for that stunt?" she asked nervously.

"Yeah, guess so. This won't be healed in time."

"Who's going to be the pilot, then?"

"Another stunt flyer, I guess. I can't imagine them sending Dylan up there with some guy who hasn't done any stunt flying. He could get Dylan killed."

Chapter 11

DYLAN WALKED THROUGH THE DOOR GRINNING. "Sorry I'm late. There was an accident on the freeway that blocked everything down through the Sepulveda Pass."

Still thinking about what Quinn had said, that he wouldn't fly with anyone but Quinn, Sonia wanted to rush into his arms and beg him not to do that helicopter stunt. Then a wave of hurt and anger washed over her as she remembered he hadn't called the night before. But that quickly broke into relief at the sight of him standing there in one piece, looking marvelous in camel slacks and a navy blue sweater that set off his eyes.

He was by her side in a moment, giving her a hug. "What's the matter, darlin'? You look pale."

The anger resurfaced and she pulled away.

"We can talk about it later—we'd better get started." Addressing everyone, she briskly explained how the experiment would work. Since Dylan and Marlee would go first, she sent Quinn and Randy into her office to wait.

As in the earlier experiment, she didn't label the cassettes so that nobody could know in which order they'd fall.

As Dylan stretched out on the bed in the adjacent room, he gave her a wink and extended his hand. "Just one kiss. It won't seem natural to be lying down on a bed without it."

"You managed quite well last night."

"Did that make you mad?"

"You have no obligation to share my bed every single night."

"It did make you mad. Good. You were thinking about me."

He had broken through her defenses. "Of course I was thinking about you! I was worried about you every minute, imagining all the things that could have gone wrong with those car hits."

"Come here. I want you to know how much I missed you."

"There isn't time."

"Sonia . . ."

Reluctantly she went to him and he pulled her down onto the bed. "I couldn't call you last night when we were out on location. There were no phones. And it was after midnight by the time I got Quinn out of the hospital, and I didn't want to wake you."

She gave him a quick kiss on the cheek. "It's okay, Dylan, really. You don't have to check in with me every minute."

He wrapped his arm tightly around her waist. "It's not a matter of obligation; it's because I want to hear the sound of your voice."

She was about to kiss him, when it struck her that with her luck, McCabe would choose that minute to walk in and then he'd really have ammunition to get her fired. She stood up quickly and smoothed her skirt. "Let's talk about this later."

"How about dinner tonight?"

She was glad he asked. "That sounds good."

"Just one thing," he said, taking her hand again. "I notice Walt isn't here."

She gave a weary sigh. "That's a long story. Tell you tonight."

Of the ten videotapes, five were of Marlee's stunts and five were Dylan's. As Sonia listened to what Dylan was saying into the microphone, noting it down on the charts, her heart raced. Marlee's hunch about their being emotionally affected by stunts seemed to be proving right.

When both teams were finished, everyone gathered in the lab to look over the charts. As she expected, Dylan and Marlee's scores were the highest. There were two instances of straight ESP in which he picked up on what she was watching, and two of precognition.

The most dramatic and irrefutable instance of precognition was a stunt in which Marlee was running through a flaming building. Dylan's voice had become agitated and raspy: "Hot, very hot, scalding . . . terrible heat and smoke. Got to get out of here."

"These results are really astonishing," Sonia said with excitement. "Forty percent is almost unheard of."

Randy and Quinn, neither of whom had ever had any sort of psychic experience, scored one correctly, and Sonia thought that was significant. The videotape was a car chase sequence from a TV show. "Fast, lots of speed and noise," Quinn had said while Randy was watching the tape. "Screeching brakes, city streets."

"So, does this prove that stuntpeople are psychic?" asked Marlee.

"That's one explanation," Sonia answered, "but it may have more to do with your being able to transmit scenes that have a strong emotional impact on you personally. I'd love to get more stuntpeople in to test out the theory."

"We'll provide you with as many as you want," offered Marlee.

"Thanks, but this is the end of the line," she said with a sad smile. "I was informed yesterday that parapsychology is being cut from the budget. Since this was already under way, I was allowed to complete it. Tomorrow they're dismantling the lab to make room for more rats."

Dylan tapped his finger angrily on the charts. "How can they cut you off in light of statistics like this? It's criminal."

"You don't know how many statistics I've

shown them. They're just not interested in psychical research."

That night Dylan came to her apartment and they made dinner together in her kitchen. Though she didn't want to be the first to bring it up, she wanted badly to broach the subject of the helicopter stunt now that Quinn was no longer the pilot. Dylan, however, seemed more interested in talking about her problems.

"Did Walt have something to do with that budget cut?" he asked as he sliced mushrooms for the salad.

"He added fuel to the fire, but it was coming anyway."

"What exactly did he say?"

"The little darling told McCabe I'd been squandering research money at the racetrack. He had pari-mutuel ticket stubs totaling over two hundred dollars."

"That creep! He didn't put that much money on my choices. I was watching him. He must have picked ticket stubs off the ground."

"He also told McCabe I was romantically involved with the subject of one of my experiments. I couldn't very well deny that, especially after he saw our Kirlian experiment Friday afternoon." She smiled up at him and handed him a ripe avocado for the salad.

"Would it make any difference if I told my version of what happened at the track?" he offered.

"I doubt it. McCabe figures you'd back me up because of our relationship, so it still comes

down to my word against Walt's. He apologized
for all the trouble he caused me, but when I
asked him to tell McCabe the truth he refused.
He was afraid it would affect his reputation."

"What about *your* reputation?"

"He's not about to consider that."

"What did McCabe say about his rat tail experiment?"

Sonia chuckled. "McCabe wouldn't hear of it.
He's canceling parapsychology, period. Even
the thought of little rodents didn't tempt him."

Dylan grated a raw carrot into the salad
and sprinkled on croutons. Then, rummaging
around in the vegetable compartment of her
refrigerator, he came up with a raw beet and
grated that in too. "I don't know who's the
bigger creep—McCabe or Walt."

"I'll vote for Walt. He's mean and under-
handed, a certifiable twerp. McCabe simply reflects the prevailing view of the scientific
establishment, which would rather ignore psychical research."

"I still think that if you showed McCabe today's results, it might change his mind."

"You don't understand the mentality I'm dealing with, Dylan. The scientific establishment is
like the church in the Middle Ages. Parapsychology is heresy. Admitting there are spooky
things like ESP and auras is the equivalent
of admitting the earth isn't the center of the
universe."

"This isn't the Dark Ages, darlin'; we've got
test-tube babies, spliced genes and space shut-
tles."

"Yes, but the basis of science is the conviction that everything in the universe is made up of matter," she explained. "If people can transmit thoughts from an isolation booth, then there's some sort of thought energy that doesn't travel on the waves of any known spectrum. It means there is a spiritual aspect to all living things and matter isn't the sole ingredient that makes up life."

"Haven't religions been preaching that for centuries? Look at the prophets in the Bible."

"Of course, but we're talking about scientists, not priests and swamis. If you accept the premise that we can see into the future, then you have to throw out all the conventional concepts of time. We're talking about scrapping the entire orderly progression of seconds, minutes, hours, days, weeks, months and years."

He poured on the oil-and-vinegar dressing and tossed the salad. "I see what you mean."

"You don't know how lucky I've been to be able to pursue psychical research as long as I have. McCabe's a real liberal compared to most university department heads."

She put the steaks in the broiler and took a sip of the chilled Bordeaux Dylan had brought.

"So what are you going to do instead of psychical research?"

"Right now I'm just worried about hanging on to my job."

Dylan's eyes narrowed. "You're getting canned because of your involvement with me?"

She rested a placating hand on his arm. "Don't feel responsible. McCabe's never liked me or my research projects. And as yet there's nothing certain about it. He said they're also going to reevaluate my performance as a professor and a therapist." She put the asparagus up to steam. "There's no use worrying about it now, anyway."

Dylan brought the sharp knife blade down on a tomato. "Damn it, but the research you're doing is important. Especially to those of us who are psychic. Half the time we're scared of it and the other half we're trying to keep it hidden so people don't think we're out of our minds. I'll bet there are people locked up on mental wards who have nothing more wrong with them than some extraordinary psychic ability. Sonia, you can't give this up."

She flipped the steaks over. "Right now, I haven't much choice."

"What if I had an isolation booth built for you at my house? We could wire it up with everything. Why do you need ULA anyway?"

"Results of backyard experiments, unfortunately, don't have the same clout as those done under the auspices of a major university. It would be next to impossible for me to get anything published in a reputable journal."

"I don't see where that would matter if you were getting results."

"Look at it this way, Dylan. It would be like your doing stunts just for your own amusement that nobody would ever see on film."

He refilled their glasses with wine. She was tired of talking about her problems and was anxious to find out what he was going to do about a new pilot.

"That was too bad about Quinn breaking his wrist," she began tentatively.

"It sure was. We just hadn't counted on that platform being so small. Fortunately, it happened during the last part of the shoot and they had enough footage to cover. How about grating some cheese for the salad?"

She inspected the salad bowl. "There's enough in there for an army. So far you've added a hard-boiled egg, a beet, a carrot, avocado, tomato, garbonzo beans, croutons, and now you want cheese?"

"There's nothing worse than a plain lettuce salad. It's like having a pizza with nothing on it but cheese and tomato sauce."

She laughed. "Oh, what the heck, throw in the cheese!"

Sonia waited until they sat down to dinner, then broached the subject again. "I guess Quinn won't be able to pilot the helicopter for that stunt now."

"You have to admit this is one superb salad, eh?" He speared a slice of avocado.

"I'm going to nominate you for Salad Maker of the Year." She was sure now he was avoiding talking about the stunt. Was it because it worried him, too?

"Are you going to hire another pilot now?"

"It's up to the stunt coordinator. I'm sure he has a long list of qualified stunt pilots."

"Will you rehearse with him?"

"If you're going to rehearse, you might as well just do the damn thing. Nobody pays you for rehearsal."

"But wouldn't that be safer?" She tried to keep her nerves in check.

"The fewer times we have to do it, the safer it is. It's a matter of cutting down on the odds of getting hurt." He put down his fork and took her hand. "Don't worry. They'll hire another experienced pilot and I'll be fine. Hey, those steaks are probably about ready. I'm going to take a look."

As he left the dining room, she tried to keep the tears from welling up. Dylan was probably putting on a brave front for her benefit and was every bit as worried as she. She remembered his saying he'd never do that stunt with anyone but Quinn.

This time she waited until they had finished dinner and were curled up on the couch with snifters of brandy before she brought up the subject again.

"Dylan, won't you reconsider doing that stunt?"

He turned her face toward him and gave her a sly look. "Don't tell me *you're* having premonitions now?"

"No, it's just a . . ." He was forcing her to admit how much it terrified her.

"You have a bad feeling about it?"

"Well, yes."

"And you had an awful feeling about the stunt work I did yesterday, too."

"Yes."

"Which leads me to believe that you would have terrible feelings about any stunt I might perform."

"Maybe you're right," she said after a moment.

He kissed her lightly. "Then trust me. I know what I'm doing or I'd be selling insurance."

She nodded halfheartedly.

"That was a delicious dinner," he said as he feathered kisses down her neck.

"It was the salad," she murmured.

"Okay, I'll take some of the credit, but you have to admit we make a good pair. I can't believe my good fortune in falling in love with a woman who can cook."

She laughed softly as she stroked his strong back. "How do you know you're in love with me? You barely know me."

"Don't you believe in love at first sight?"

"Not at all."

"You felt nothing the first time you saw me?"

"I was wildly attracted," she admitted. "But I wouldn't call it love."

"How much longer do you need before you know for sure?"

She checked her watch. "At least another fifteen minutes, maybe twenty."

It was still too soon to be certain of love—it had to be. How could he speak of love so soon? She did know that she liked him immensely as a person and that those feelings grew stronger the more she was with him.

What gnawed at her was his profession. Could

she deal with that fear every time he went out to do an ordinary car hit? How did the spouses of policemen and -women cope with it?

She rested her cheek against his chest and closed her eyes. After worrying all last night, it was good to have his arms safely around her again.

"Hey, my darling shrink, you're nodding off on me. Why don't we go to bed?"

He lifted her in his powerful arms and took her to the bedroom. "I think I'm getting swept off my feet again by a tall, dark, handsome man."

"That's what you get for hanging around with fortune-tellers. Hey, sweet gypsy, you do look sleepy," he said as he set her down on the bed. He unbuttoned her blouse and kissed the tip of each breast.

She sighed with pleasure and ran her fingers through his thick black hair, gratefully letting him remove her clothes. As he ran his large hands lovingly over her body, the sleepiness began to dissolve. Everywhere he touched her, her skin felt as if it were being electrified.

Lying back against the pillows, she watched him undress and marveled again at the beauty of his physique. In a moment the lights were out and he was beside her in the bed.

"You won't fall asleep on me, now will you?" he teased.

"I won't promise . . . Oh, Dylan . . ."

As he caressed the silky insides of her thighs, she felt herself beginning to lose control. Then suddenly sparks began shooting through her at such a rapid rate that all she could do was give herself over to him.

From her lips strange animal sounds came that she didn't recognize as her own. She wanted desperately to return the pleasure he was giving her, but she was unable to disengage herself from the trembling ecstasies.

Just when she was sure she could stand no more, new waves of delight flowed through her as he entered her.

"Dylan . . ."

He was smiling down at her. "Your eyes are so dark and luminous, so black when you're making love."

He thrust into her again, this time going deeper. "Do you like this?" he said huskily.

She gasped and shuddered around him. "Mmmm. Quite a stunt."

He grinned. "We're going to be doing a lot of stunts together from now on."

"Not the trapeze."

"No? The highwire then?"

"I already feel like I'm on a high, high wire, a million miles out in space."

When they finally finished touring the stratosphere, Sonia slipped into a deep and unfettered sleep in his arms.

The helicopter hovered over the red convertible. "You worked up your nerve to go down there yet?" the pilot spat out sarcastically.

Dylan didn't have much confidence in this

replacement for Quinn. Something about the smirking malevolence in the man's eyes made Dylan cringe.

"Watch that you don't drop down too low," Dylan told him as he started onto the ladder.

The smirk turned to a scowl. "Look, Mario, don't be telling me how to do my job."

Dylan froze.

"Go on, Mario. What's stopping you, kid?" he taunted. "Your little friend Sonia's down there, you know."

He felt a mounting rage. "Why aren't they using Marlee?"

"I had them replace her with your beloved Sonia."

"You bastard, you'll get her killed. I'm not going down there."

"You'd better, kid. That's the only way she can escape." He knew his father well enough to know he meant what he said.

Malicious laughter followed him as he made his way down the ladder and hung upside down on the trapeze bar.

The whole stunt was rigged. Sonia—beautiful, black-haired, gypsy-eyed woman. How he loved her. He'd never loved any woman like this before. Why did his father want to kill her? Why did his father do anything? There was no time to think about it. He had to get her out of that convertible.

Her face was stricken with fear as she reached up to him. "Trust me, darlin'," he said over and over again, but he wasn't sure he could get her out safely. Maybe it was wrong to *ask her to trust him when his love for her was what had put her in this danger.*

She grabbed his wrists, but her hold wasn't tight enough. She was slipping back into the car.

Before he could get another grip on her the helicopter moved to the left and began dropping him down.

"You're too low, dammit!" he shouted at his father, but the noise of the rotors was too loud, and Dylan knew it would make no difference even if he could hear.

He could see the rear hubcap spinning beside him . . . then his head slammed onto the pavement. Sonia was calling his name. Poor beautiful gypsy-eyed. . .

"Dylan. Dylan, darling. Wake up. It's okay. You were dreaming."

"Sonia?" He ran his hands over her body. "You don't know how good you feel."

"Was it the nightmare again?" She touched his forehead. It was damp.

"Yeah. It was a little different this time."

"Tell me about this one."

He kissed her cheek. "Let's wait until morning. You were so tired. I don't want to keep you up."

"I won't fall asleep unless I know what was in the dream," she protested. "You have a dream interpreter right here in your bed. Might as well take advantage of her."

He took a deep breath and began. "Quinn wasn't the pilot in this one."

"That makes sense. You just found out he wouldn't be. Who was the pilot?"

"My dad."

"At the controls," she pointed out while running a soothing hand down his chest.

"You were in the car again. He told me that he'd put you down there, and I was sure he did it because he wanted to kill you."

"Two impossibilities there as far as precognition," she noted. "Your dad would never be piloting, and I would never be in that car."

"Not unless you picked up a union card," he joked.

"Sure, Dylan."

"Or you did it on a waver."

She chuckled. "No way, my darling. What else happened in the dream? Did you go down on the ladder this time?"

"Yes. I was close enough to see you were terrified, and I kept telling you to trust me even though I wondered if you should since I was the one who put you in danger. You tried to grip my wrists, but you slipped out. Then the helicopter dropped me off to the side of the car and I went down on the pavement."

She turned the details of the dream over in her mind. "Okay, let's go over this. First of all, your father in both dreams was in a position of authority, just as he was in real life. He could make life-or-death decisions about you."

"And about you, Sonia. That's what I don't understand—how you got pulled into this."

"I'm sleeping beside you; I'm on your mind.

That's one explanation. Who was the girl before?"

"Marlee—just like it will be in the stunt. But my father wasn't in those other dreams. That's just happened since I met you. The only detail that remained the same was my getting slammed into the pavement."

"Do you remember what your father did to your dog?"

"What's that got to do with anything?"

"You're associating me with your dog."

He laughed and fluffed her hair playfully. "I don't want to disappoint you, darlin', but you don't bear the slightest resemblance. Well, maybe the ears."

"But you cared a lot for the dog."

"I loved that mutt."

"And your father callously took the one thing you cared about and destroyed it."

He rested his chin on top of her head. "That does make sense. In the dream I kept thinking about how much I loved you and how unfair it was that he could do this to you."

She caressed him softly. "Dylan, it's like how I hold myself back from love out of fear something disastrous will happen as a consequence."

He brushed her cheek with the backs of his fingers. "You still afraid of falling in love with me?"

She turned her head and kissed the tips of his fingers. "I care for you, Dylan, more than I've ever cared for anyone, but I need more time."

"You've got until tomorrow morning." He

stretched and yawned, settling back onto the pillows. "The only thing that still makes me think there might be a trace of precognition is how, in every dream, the helicopter drops down and my head hits the pavement."

"First of all, that's a very real possibility. But maybe when you were a kid your father held you upside down and dropped you on the pavement."

"He usually came after me in the house."

"Well, maybe you don't remember now, but it's still in your subconscious and the stunt triggered it."

"You're probably right. Anyway, I feel better. Now I understand why people see shrinks." He wrapped himself around her. "Nice to have one in my bed."

In moments she heard his deep, even breathing and was confident he'd get through the night without another bad dream. She felt his muscles relax and had the satisfaction of knowing she had been on target. These were the moments that made her work worthwhile.

Only one thing nagged her: the recurring detail of his head hitting the pavement. She only hoped it was nothing more than a suppressed, terrifying memory from a brutal childhood.

Chapter 12

THE NEXT MORNING SONIA SLIPPED OUT OF BED quietly so as not to disturb Dylan's sleep. With the covers half off, his tanned body made a dramatic contrast with the bright yellow sheets. A surge of affection for him filled her.

Unable to resist, she returned to the bedside and sat down beside him. Just one more moment to study the face whose contours she had traced so lovingly the night before. It was craggy now, with a dark morning beard. His black eyelashes seemed absurdly long on his cheeks, and his hair was tousled on the pillow. It was a hard, angular face, but when he slept it mellowed.

Sensing he was being watched, he stirred and opened his eyes. His voice was gravelly with sleep. "What are you doing up, gypsy lady? Come back to bed." He encircled her waist and rested his head on her thighs.

"I've got to teach an eight o'clock class," she said softly while stroking his hair.

"What can I do to induce you to climb back into bed?"

"Save your strength. I can't afford to add skipped classes to the long list of my other heretical sins."

He nibbled provocatively on her thigh. "I like a woman with heretical sins." He rolled over on his back and, reaching up through her long, dark hair, pulled her face down to his. "Kiss me goodbye and I'll let you go."

She complied without objection, lingering longer than she had intended. "All right, now I've got to go."

"What time are you through today?"

"Around six."

"My place tonight?"

"Dylan, don't you think we're rushing things a bit?"

"Definitely."

"Then maybe we should take a night away from each other."

"We did that the other night and you weren't happy about it at all. What's changed?"

"Dylan, we need some time away to sort out our feelings."

"Mine are all sorted. I want you every minute you can spare. For all I know you might go into work this morning and become passionately enamored of a handsome, square-jawed psychologist who runs rats through mazes. And then where would that leave us?"

His tone was light, but there was something in the depths of his eyes that revealed what did worry him. It wasn't a rival he thought would steal her away from him, but his own death. He'd spent most of his life cheating it, first with his father, then the circus, and then Vietnam. And now, because of the nightmare, he was afraid it might beat him.

"Are you cooking tonight?" she asked, kissing the tip of his nose.

"I'm afraid my culinary expertise begins and ends with salads. I thought I'd take you out to dinner. How do you feel about Thai food?"

"Love it."

"Good, there's a wonderful little place not far from my house. Why don't you come by as soon as you're finished at the hospital?"

She leaned down and kissed him again. "Sounds like a delicious idea." He started to sit up, but she stopped him. "No reason for you to leave. Why not stay here and sleep for a while?"

He glanced around the room and yawned. "Not a bad idea." He pulled a pillow under his head, but instead of drifting back off to sleep he watched her get ready. Soon his intense gaze began to make her self-conscious.

"Why don't you go back to sleep?" she said.

"After you leave. I'm enjoying the show."

"Watching me brush my hair?"

"One of the most beautiful things I've ever seen in my life."

She started to laugh, then saw that he was serious.

"Every movement you make is unique and beautiful and very sexy—the way you smooth your stockings over your legs; the way you put on your lipstick."

When she was about to go, he called after her, "Reconsider talking to McCabe about our precognition experiments."

She sighed defeatedly. "Oh, Dylan, I'd love to, for your sake as much as mine. But it's like banging my head against a stone wall. He'd only turn me down."

"Try," he said as he slipped back down under the covers.

"No, darling. It's a noble thought, but I'm afraid it's a lost cause."

The helicopter was lowering him down. He could see Sonia in the back seat of the convertible. And oddly, she wasn't afraid. She watched him calmly as he descended. "It's okay, Dylan," she said as she reached up to him. "I trust you now."

Their hands were almost touching. "Nothing to it," he said to her. She smiled as she took a firm grip of his wrists and he began lifting her out. This was the most dangerous part, getting her clear of the car.

Then suddenly the helicopter shifted over. He let go of her wrists just in time and she dropped back into the car. He shouted at the pilot, but he couldn't be heard over the noise of the blades. The pilot was dropping him down lower. He was level with the rear wheel; the pavement was looming up at him. Then he hit.

Dylan woke up in a sweat, the pillow knotted in his fist. Looking around, he realized he was in Sonia's bedroom. The scent of her perfume was still fresh on the pillow.

He began to relax and tried to think about how Sonia would analyze the dream. At least his father wasn't in this one, but what did it mean that the stuntwoman was still Sonia . . . something about her trusting him? Was he wishing that she could love him? He looked longingly at her pillow. Damn, but there was never a shrink in your bed when you needed one.

How much analysis would it take before these nightmares stopped? He didn't have that much time. It would be suicide to go out there and perform the stunt with his mind muddled up like this. Marlee's life depended on his having his faculties sharp.

The only solution he could see was hypnosis. Why not? Sonia couldn't do her experiments anyway, and he made enough money now so that he didn't have to depend on the horse races.

When she came over that night, he'd ask her to do it. Then maybe he could get a good night's sleep.

As Sonia drove to work, her thoughts drifted back to the nightmare. Had she been wrong in explaining it to him as a bad dream with psychological overtones? What if it really were a protective psychic mechanism issuing him a warning? She wondered if maybe she should be trying harder to talk him out of doing the stunt. But it wasn't likely he'd listen, and she didn't want to risk having her fears make him more nervous.

As soon as her class was over she went back to her office. As she was passing her lab, she saw Walt Anguin already beginning to dismantle the Kirlian camera. She couldn't bear to watch. It was like witnessing an execution.

She shut herself in her office, and although she had papers to correct, she found herself drawn to the charts from yesterday's experiments. The results were remarkable, but she desperately needed more statistics from Dylan to make the study publishable.

In some of the experiments she'd done with ESP, she found that the longer people stayed with it, the better they performed in a laboratory environment. It could be the same with Dylan. With practice, his scores might even increase to an unheard-of eighty, even a hundred percent.

She thought about how much the research meant to Dylan and other people with the same gifts. For his sake, if for nothing else, she should give it a fight. There had to be a way to convince McCabe.

With sudden steely resolve, she stuffed all the charts into a manila folder and stormed into McCabe's office.

"I want to see Dr. McCabe," she told the secretary without stopping to catch her breath.

"He's in his lab." The secretary was unimpressed by Sonia's urgency. "Is it important?"

"Extremely. Can you get him on the phone for me?"

"He said not to disturb him for anything unless it's a matter of life or death."

"That's exactly what it is. I need him to grant a stay of execution."

"Really, Dr. Barnes." The secretary smiled weakly at what she thought was a joke.

"If you won't call him, I'm going straight to his lab," she threatened.

"You can't just go barging in there!"

"No? Watch me."

Throwing all caution to the wind, Sonia flew down the hall with the secretary calling after her, "He'll kill you!"

McCabe's lab was easy to recognize by the forbidding sign on the door: KEEP OUT! MICE ON TEMPERATURE CONTROL!

That was a direct enough order, but not as strong as her conviction. She had to talk to him now before she lost her isolation booth. Clenching her teeth, she opened the door and slipped quietly inside.

McCabe and an assistant, both in white coats, were taking a rat from a cage. They turned at the sound of her high heels on the floor.

"Dr. Barnes," he bellowed. "What the hell are you doing in here? Can't you read signs?"

"Yes, but I had to talk to you immediately." Thinking of Dylan, she lifted her chin and said bravely, "If you'll just give me a few minutes to show you something, I'll explain."

McCabe's beady eyes were bulging in rage. His hand shook as he placed the squirming rat back in the cage.

With McCabe's furious gaze pinned on her, she had a sudden attack of trepidation. He was a man who liked appointments made well in advance. But she had come this far and he hadn't kicked her out. Not yet, anyway. What did she have to lose, her job? That was nearly lost anyway.

He beckoned her over to a lab table away from his assistant. "What is so important that you would interrupt my lab work?" he said angrily.

She spread the charts out in front of him and carefully explained the results of her experiments. To her amazement, he didn't crumple them up and toss them in the nearest garbage can. In fact, he even began to nod his head in short jerks and punctuate the nods with an odd guttural sound she hoped signified approval.

"This is quite extraordinary," he said finally.

She managed a tentative smile. "Dr. McCabe, if I had a few more months to study Dylan Hamlin and these other stuntpeople, I think the results would be well worth the time."

"I don't know what you're going to get from these other stuntpeople, but Mr. Hamlin's consistent performance under controlled lab conditions is truly astonishing. Would he be willing to do more experiments with us?"

"Yes, I know he would. He's very anxious to go ahead with it."

McCabe readjusted his horn-rimmed glasses as he pored over the charts. "I'd suggest you continue using other stuntmen as controls, but I'd like to see you try Hamlin and his partner with videotapes of stunts he's never seen before, as well as more of those he's done."

She held her breath. "Are you telling me to go ahead with the study?"

"It kills me, Dr. Barnes, because basically I think precognition is bunk. But I can't deny this."

Sonia suppressed a strong desire to throw her arms around the balding, beady-eyed man and kiss him. Instead, she said with quiet dignity, "Thank you, Dr. McCabe. Er, could you call down to my lab and make sure Walt leaves the isolation booth intact?"

He made another guttural sound she was now sure meant an affirmative and picked up the telephone. Sonia gathered up her papers as quietly as possible and, not wanting to press her luck any further, made for the door.

She was barely through it when McCabe's voice boomed after her. "And Dr. Barnes . . ."

"Yes?"

"Don't ever disturb me in my lab again unless it's a matter of life or death."

If she hadn't been afraid they'd lock her in a ward upstairs, she would have tap-danced all the way down the corridor, she was so ecstatically happy.

The first thing to do was call Dylan and tell him. He was the only one who would be as excited as she. She quickly dialed his number and was disappointed to reach his answering device. Not wanting to leave her exciting message on a machine, she hung up. It was unlikely he'd still be sleeping at her place, but just in case, she called anyway. There was no answer. Well, she'd see him after work. It would be much more fun to tell him in person and see the look on his face.

In the meantime she called Marlee, who was thrilled with the news. "You don't know how glad I am," Marlee bubbled. "After I left the other day, I kept thinking it was a shame you couldn't continue with your work. It's so good for Dylan to finally have some scientific evidence to back him up. I think it's been real hard for him at times to live with all that psychic stuff. Have you talked to him yet?"

"I tried to call him but he wasn't home. I'm going there right after work, so I'll tell him in person. That'll be more fun anyway."

"You bet. Hey, in the meantime, would you like me to call some more stuntpeople for you?"

"Yes. In fact, that's one of the reasons I called. You were gracious enough to offer the other day."

"I'll get on the phone right away to my friends and have them call you."

"I'd really appreciate it."

"No problem. This is exciting for me, too. It's the first time in my life I've ever felt I was contributing to something important. Entertaining people with stunts isn't exactly in the same category as finding a cure for cancer."

"This isn't either," said Sonia.

"Maybe, but it's a heck of a lot closer."

Sonia floated through the afternoon so happily she didn't even mind the bumper-to-bumper rush hour traffic on the freeway to Dylan's house. It gave her pleasure to imagine how he'd look when she told him about her reprieve. Dylan was the one to thank for making it possible. It was his precognition that had impressed McCabe.

When he opened the door, her pulse jumped as it always did at the magnificent sight of him. But the moment he enfolded her in his strong arms she sensed something was wrong.

"Dylan, what is it?"

He pulled away from her and crossed the room. Whatever he had to say was difficult. "This morning after you left, I went back to sleep and . . ."

Her heart stopped, but she tried not to show it. "The dream again?"

"At least my father wasn't in it this time. But you were still the stuntwoman."

She sat down on the couch so he wouldn't notice her legs were shaky. "Well, let's discuss it and find the key," she said, mustering her professional calm. "Tell me from beginning to end exactly what was in the dream. Who was the pilot?"

He shook his head. "No, Sonia. We've gone as far as we can with dream analysis. We get one aspect of it figured out and I just come up with a new twist. I want you to hypnotize me."

"You're sure about that? What about the horse races and the . . ." She had to stop herself from telling him about McCabe. The last thing she wanted was to influence him on her behalf. If he felt he needed the hypnosis, then she would give it to him.

"It's like I told you when I first came to your office. I can't have this muddling up my mind when I do that stunt next week. Marlee's life depends on my being able to pull her out of that car safely and hang on to her as we make the ascent."

"All right then, let's go ahead. Why don't you sit in that armchair by the window." She turned out all the lights so that the only light source would be the setting sun coming through the window behind him.

"Now I want you to relax." Her voice was low and calming as she went around behind him. She stroked gently downward from the top of his head to his shoulders. "You see that saber over the mantel? I want you to focus on that, nothing else. If your eyes get tired, go ahead and close them."

She continued stroking for a while; then, feeling him start to relax, she moved around in front of him. He was already having a hard time keeping his eyes open. "Now I want you to think about your toes. Picture them in your mind; wiggle them around. Relax them one by one; feel all the tension leave them." She waited a moment, then continued. "Now your ankles. Let all the tension float away."

As she continued to work her way up his body

with her suggestions, she marveled at his self-control. Few people were that in tune with their bodies. Experience had taught him how to manipulate each muscle.

She was lucky that he'd had so much practice putting himself into a trance and that he trusted her so completely.

"You are floating on a white fluffy cloud in a vast blue sky." Her voice was soft and soothing. "Not a care in the world. Floating, floating. You are feeling sleepy and resting peacefully. You hear nothing but my voice."

The face muscles that had been so tightly drawn when she walked into the room now eased. "Imaginé hundreds of blue balloons attached to your right hand, lifting your hand up higher and higher without your doing anything at all." She was gratified to see his hand begin to lift from the elbow at the suggestion. "When your hand is all the way up, I'm going to count backward from ten to one. When I reach one you are going to be in a deep trance. You'll continue to hear my voice and you'll remember everything I say to you."

His right arm continued to lift, and when it was vertical she counted slowly. She saw his eyelids flutter. "Now I want you to imagine that your hand is made of lead." His hand plummeted back down to the arm of the chair.

Satisfied he was under and receptive, she began talking about his precognition. "From now on you'll continue to have premonitions, but they'll occur only in dreams, and they won't disturb you. You'll sleep through them peacefully, and when you wake up in the morning, you won't even remember them."

While he was under hypnosis she was tempted to take him back to his childhood to see if he could remember his father dropping him on the pavement, but reawakening memories of his father would put him in a state of agitation, and that wouldn't help him right now. Since he was such a good subject, perhaps he'd be willing to let her do it another time.

She also thought about his wanting to retain the power of picking winners at the track, but that, too, could complicate the hypnotic suggestion.

"When you awaken, you'll remember everything I've said and you're going to feel wonderful, extremely rested and in good spirits, as though you've just had a good night's sleep." She let him stay relaxed a while longer, then said, "Dylan, I'm going to count to ten, and when I say 'ten' you'll wake up."

When she finished, he blinked his eyes open and smiled at her. "Thanks."

She came over to him and he pulled her down on his lap, wrapping his arms around her. "I had no idea hypnosis was like that. It's a wonderful feeling."

"You're one of the easiest subjects I've ever had. You have marvelous self-control."

He kissed her neck. "I'm quickly losing it."

Just as she was beginning to respond to his kisses there was a knock at the door.

"That must be Marlee," he said, lifting Sonia

off his lap. "She left a message on my machine that she'd be stopping by but didn't say why."

Sonia froze. Marlee was bound to say something about the experiment. How was she going to stop her?

Marlee rushed in with a hug for Dylan and a hug for her, a bottle of chilled champagne in her hand. "Dylan, isn't it exciting?"

He gave her a quizzical look. "Isn't what exciting? What's the champagne for?"

Marlee clapped a hand over her mouth. "Oh, no, you haven't told him yet. Sonia, I'm so sorry! I know you wanted to be the one to give him the good news."

He turned on Sonia. "What good news?"

"It's nothing, really." She tried to warn Marlee with her eyes to drop the subject.

"Oh, Sonia, you're so modest. Well, I've already spilled this much of the beans, I might as well spill the rest. Sonia showed her boss the experiments we did the other day, and he was so impressed with your performance on precognition that he's letting her continue. If it hadn't been for you, she'd never have been able to do it!"

All his muscles, which had been so relaxed only moments ago, were now coiled with fury.

"Why didn't you tell me?"

"I didn't want it to influence you."

His eyes grew wild. "Damn you."

"What's wrong with you?" Marlee scolded him. "You should be congratulating Sonia, not raking her over the coals."

"It wasn't fair not to let me know," he snapped.

"I had no choice."

"There is always a choice."

"You would never have gone through the hypnosis if I'd told you."

"Exactly."

"I don't understand," complained Marlee. "What's going on?"

"Sonia just hypnotized me to get rid of my precognitions."

Marlee's mouth fell open. "Why in the world would you want to be rid of something most people would give their eye teeth to have? Think of all that money you're always winning at the racetrack!"

He gazed at Marlee for a long moment, but he didn't tell her she was at the crux of his decision. Sonia knew he couldn't bear to make Marlee feel responsible any more than Sonia would have burdened him with guilt over having to give up her experiments. Instead he turned back to Sonia. "You know that research meant as much to me as it did to you. You led me to believe there was no possibility of it continuing."

She leaned against the wall and closed her eyes. "I didn't really think McCabe would change his mind, but this morning, as I watched Walt dismantling the equipment, a kind of rage came over me. I stormed into McCabe's rat lab and practically shoved my charts down his throat. But you don't have to feel all is lost simply because you won't be doing the experiments. It's no big deal, Dylan. Remember that Randy and Quinn each had one good instance of ESP, and there may be other stuntpeople who can . . ."

He stepped toward her, and with his thumb under her chin, he forced her to look into his eyes. "But with me you would have been assured of precognition. If you get it again, it's going to be sheer luck and you know it."

She also knew that it was only because of Dylan's success with precognition that McCabe had allowed her to continue. Without him, her experiments would be over.

"Hey, listen, you guys," Marlee broke in, brushing some blond curls from her forehead. "This is no way to behave. Besides, I have something else important to tell you. I was kind of hoping we could make a general celebration out of it."

Dylan and Sonia temporarily forgot their discussion and regarded her with questioning anticipation.

"I don't know quite how to tell you," she said uneasily. "I hope you won't be mad."

"You just said it was a matter for celebration," he reminded her.

"Frank—he's the guy I've been living with," she explained to Sonia. "He was working as an A.D.—that's an assistant director—and he just got a chance to direct an episode of *The Dream Machine*. It was a real stroke of luck. The producer's wife and I are in the same exercise class, and we all ended up going out to dinner one night and—"

"That's great for Frank," said Dylan. "Come on, let's open that champagne. We need something good to celebrate." He started to unwrap the cork. "Now, what were you afraid I'd be mad about?"

Marlee took a deep breath. "You see, the script calls for a blond actress who's a gymnast, and so of course they right away thought of me. It's not the lead, but it's a big role with a lot of dimension, more than anything I've ever done before. I went to audition this afternoon. I think they liked the fact that they wouldn't need a double for the gymnastic stuff, so I got the part."

Dylan popped the cork and it flew across the room, hitting a blunderbuss above the mantel. "Marlee, that's sensational. It's just the kind of break you've needed."

"Congratulations," said Sonia warmly.

Dylan went into the kitchen and emerged with three champagne glasses. After they toasted her success, he said, "So why in the world should I be mad at you?"

Marlee gulped down some champagne and wrinkled her tiny nose at the bubbles. "The second day of shooting falls on the same day we were supposed to do that helicopter stunt. I don't want to cancel out on you after all our preparation, but then again . . ."

"Don't be crazy. You do the *The Dream Machine*. I'll find someone else to do the stunt."

Sonia couldn't swallow the champagne, nor could she meet Dylan's eyes. Quinn was no longer pilot, Marlee no longer the stuntwoman. One by one the elements of the dream were coming together with the precision of a lab experiment.

Chapter 13

MARLEE FINISHED HER GLASS OF CHAMPAGNE, then apologized for having to leave. "Frank and I are attending a screening tonight at the Directors' Guild."

There was an awkward silence after she left. Dylan poured them both another glass of champagne, but the festive mood had vanished with Marlee.

Dylan downed his glass quickly and said, "I don't know about you, but I'm starving to death. You ready to go to dinner?"

"I've been thinking about that Thai dinner all day."

She was charmed by the tiny neighborhood restaurant where the husband was chef and the wife and children waited on tables. They all greeted Dylan like an old friend.

Like an invisible monster, the subject of the stunt lay sleeping between them. Neither of them was willing to wake it up. Searching for a neutral topic, Sonia said pleasantly, "It's nice to see a family united together to work like this."

"For the Chans, it's an economic necessity," he shot back. "He'd never be able to afford to run the restaurant if the family weren't helping out."

Dylan's antagonistic tone surprised her, but it seemed to reflect the tension between them. "Even so, the kids are going to grow up with a strong sense of belonging," she argued. "It gives them all something in common. My mother was a real estate broker, my father an accountant. We all went our separate ways, and on the odd night we all ended up at the dinner table together, we found ourselves staring at each other without much to say."

"A family-run business can also be a trap," Dylan pointed out. "I saw that in the circus. In the Colombo family, everyone had to be a horseman. One of the kids was afraid of horses, and it grew into an impossible situation."

Sonia took a bite of a delicious hors d'oeuvre and tried to remember that she'd come into the restaurant with an appetite. "Why do you feel you have to dispute everything I say?"

"I'm not disputing," he said testily. "We're having a friendly discussion about the pros and cons of family businesses."

"You don't sound very friendly."

He put his chopsticks down and reached for her hand. "Sonia, what's really bothering you?"

She pulled her hand away from his. "I just wonder if we haven't been trying to create an illusion, kind of like car hits. You know—how the audience thinks the car is hitting you but you're actually hitting the car? We're deluding ourselves into believing we're falling in love, when actually—"

"We *are* falling in love," he said. "Why the negatives all of a sudden?"

She pushed the food around her plate with the end of a chopstick. "Do you remember the reactions of our auras on the Kirlian photography?"

"Visual proof of what's going on between us."

"Yes, but all those flaming sparks aren't enough to sustain a relationship when two people aren't of the same temperament."

"It sounds to me like you're just fishing for excuses. If you want to end it, just say so."

"I don't want to end it."

He gave her a sharp look. "Then what do you want to do?"

"Dammit, Dylan, I don't want it to continue, either." She wanted to tell him how frightened she was now that Marlee had also canceled out on the stunt, but she was afraid her fears would affect him.

"What's bugging you?"

"You're a very active physical person," she hedged, "and I'm absolutely gutless."

He pinned her with a direct gaze she couldn't avoid and sat back in his chair. "We're like a couple of Victorians too timid to talk about sex. Marlee's canceling scared you. That's the basis of this, isn't it?"

"Is there anything I can say to change your mind about doing that stunt?"

"No."

"Well then, why bother to discuss it?" she said angrily. "Maybe it would be better just to end it."

"Using another stuntwoman isn't going to increase my danger. In fact, I'll probably do better with someone I have no emotional ties to."

"What are you going to do about finding a replacement?"

"Make some phone calls in the morning. There are dozens of unemployed stuntwomen around."

"Who would do that kind of stunt?"

"I'd probably have to train someone, but that won't take long. All she needs is a good grip and confidence that I won't drop her. You could even do it."

"Dylan!"

"Calm down, honey. I was just kidding." He brushed the backs of his fingers across her cheek. "I'd never let you do it. That's one part of the dream that can't possibly come true. Now eat something, or you're going to embarrass me with the Chans."

They finished the meal in an uneasy truce, steering their conversation to neutral topics picked from the news.

In the car on the way back to his house, he

joked, "You said we didn't have much in common, but we both feel the same way about the nuclear freeze, anchovies, the budget deficit and Thai food. What more do you want?"

She drew lazy figure eights on his thigh. "Do you suppose our astrological signs are compatible?"

"Do you believe in that stuff?"

"No."

"Neither do I. Have you ever done any research on astrology?"

"The Russians claim that people who were born during high sunspot activity have more psychic ability, but I don't see much basis for the rest. Stars and planets may have some magnetic pull on us, but just because somebody connects the dots on a star chart to make drawings of lions and centaurs doesn't mean those constellations have any control over my life."

Dylan agreed. "It's like making predictions on the basis of what some clever artist drew on playing cards, or the ancient practice of disemboweling sheep to read their livers, or interpreting omens."

"It sounds like you've done some research into clairvoyance."

"Zenobia had a whole library on the subject in her trailer."

"I've spoken to some psychics who use a crystal ball. Did you ever see anything in hers?"

"No, but then, it was plastic."

Sonia laughed. "I don't know that it would make any difference. I think it may work because staring at an object puts you into a receptive trance, like I did with you yesterday, having you focus on the saber."

"What fascinated me was the use of mirrors in fortune-telling," he said. "Did you ever wonder why mermaids were always pictured holding hand mirrors?"

"Vanity?"

"No. They were connected with the goddess Aphrodite, and her priestesses used to look into mirrors to see the future."

"Oh, like the witch in 'Snow White' saying, 'Mirror, mirror on the wall.' I'd love to have had you look into a real crystal ball. It would have been an interesting experiment."

His expression darkened as he pulled in the driveway and stopped the car. "Damn, but I wish now you hadn't hypnotized me. We could have done all kinds of experiments."

"Dylan," she said as he unlocked the front door, "would you do another experiment for me?"

"What would be the point?"

She followed him into the living room, where he lit a fire in the fireplace. "It would be a way of checking to see if the hypnosis worked."

"You mean like a before-and-after test?"

"At least if someone ever came to me with that problem again, I'd have something to go on."

"Let's do it next week."

"Before or after the stunt?"

"Before. That way, if I have another nightmare, I'll know what I'm dealing with."

He put Bach's *Brandenburg* Concertos on the stereo and they sank down on the couch in front of the fire. She watched the flames dance in time to the music and tried not to think about next week. The monster seemed to hover near as she made love to him that night, blanketing them like a fog as they fell asleep.

But there were no nightmares.

Sunlight poured into the spacious bedroom through the tall arched windows. Sonia was just beginning to stir awake in Dylan's arms and was musing that, even though she must have moved around during the night, they awoke in the same position in which they'd fallen asleep.

The telephone jarred her fully awake. She grabbed for it automatically; then, remembering where she was, she handed it to Dylan.

He pressed it to his ear, cleared his throat, and without opening his eyes mumbled, "Yes."

His eyes shot open and a muscle in his jaw tightened. "What? The hell I will. Forget it!"

He sat up abruptly with all his senses keen, his body coiled and tense. "No, dammit, I'm not going to work with just any chopper pilot. I don't care what war he was in. I was over there too, and I saw a hell of a lot of blithering idiots flying helicopters. What the hell does this guy know about stunt flying?"

Sonia listened anxiously, barely able to breathe.

He got out of bed and paced back and forth with the telephone in his hand. "There has to be an experienced stunt pilot available. Didn't you talk to Quinn? He knows everybody in the business. By the way, Marlee Elden had to cancel. . . . No, I'll call around myself. . . . Okay, talk to you later today."

Dylan slammed down the receiver and got back into bed. She was glad for the comfort and warmth of his body again, but it didn't take away the fear. "Aren't they going to use a regular stunt pilot?"

"The stunt coordinator assured me the pilot he hired can pull it off."

She glanced over at the clock. "Don't you think you should start calling around for stuntwomen?"

"First things first." He pulled her down on top of him and claimed her mouth in a kiss that made her temporarily forget the frightening phone call and everything else but the warmth of his strong body.

Feeling his hard insistence, she opened herself to him and let his passion fill her.

She loved his morning look, disheveled and raw, the turquoise eyes heavy-lidded. She ran her fingers through the dark hair of his chest and watched the lazy smile begin on his lips.

Now that she knew the movements and rhythms he liked, she enjoyed teasing him with them, hearing the deep sounds of pleasure that came from his lips.

If only they could make love like this indefinitely and shut out the world. Throwing back her black mane, she rode him with a fury he couldn't seem to get enough of. It was as though they had to pack all the love and passion into these few moments, as though they had only a little time left.

Dylan began calling stuntwomen at the breakfast table. She was amused to hear his end of a few conversations. Though he did his best to keep it from her, it was obvious he'd been intimately involved with some of them.

"It sounds to me like you've done more than just work with some of these stuntwomen," she said slyly.

"Sometimes when you're on location, well, you know . . ." He shrugged. "It's no big thing. We all stay friendly. It's like family."

"It does sound as though you've kept them all as very good friends."

He took her hand and kissed the palm. "I figured out a long time ago that it wasn't worth it to make love to someone you didn't like a lot. Coming to grips with that in the morning is worse than waking up with a nasty hangover."

"Did you ever have an affair with Marlee?"

He was in the midst of dialing another number and put down the receiver. "Yes."

Sonia felt a pang of jealousy. A faceless stuntwoman at the other end of the telephone line was one thing, but Marlee she could visualize.

Then suddenly she knew why Dylan had reacted differently at the mention of Marlee. "When you told me you had been in love, you were talking about her, weren't you?"

He nodded and took a long sip of coffee.

Sonia didn't like being thrown into competition with the vivacious young woman. "What happened?"

"You remember the story about the Greek sculptor who fell in love with 'the statue he created? It was something like that. She was a skinny kid from a broken home who lived not far from here, hanging out with punk motorcycle types. I got her started on the trampoline and parallel bars. Pretty soon she was competing in gymnastic events in high school. I taught her what I could about stunts, and she worked harder than anybody I'd ever seen. Then one day I noticed she was twenty, gorgeous and seductive as hell—and spending the nights here.

"What I didn't understand was the difference between good friendship with good sex thrown in, and love. Fortunately, she did and called a halt."

"Do you think she was just using you to break into the stunt business?"

"She was, in a way, just like she's using Frank. It's not coldhearted scheming. I happen to know she's crazy about the guy, but it doesn't hurt that he's in a good position to get her work. Marlee's one of the most fiercely loyal people I've ever met. I was in a car accident a few years ago doing a stunt for a TV cop show. She was at the hospital day and night, then stayed here at the house for a week after I got home. Frank wasn't too happy about it, but she wouldn't budge until she knew I was okay." He filled their cups with more coffee. "I wanted to tell you before, but I wasn't sure how you'd take it."

"I'm glad you told me," she said softly. "I don't want any secrets between us."

He resumed his calling. One stuntwoman had a broken collarbone; another had already lined up another job that day.

The last one recommended a friend who agreed to do it. Dylan asked her to come by that afternoon so they could work on the trapeze for practice.

"She's just starting out," said Dylan as he hung up the phone, "but she's done some gymnastics and acrobatics."

"How'd she feel about swinging from a helicopter a hundred fifty feet in the air?"

"She wasn't crazy about it, but said she could use the money. I suppose if she panics I could always use a dummy up there for the long shot."

"If that's the case, why don't they rig up dummies for both of you?"

"One of us has got to be real or it won't look natural."

"Do you really think people would know the difference?"

He shrugged. "Hanging up there isn't the hard part, anyway. It's getting the helicopter steady over the car to pull the girl out."

She thought of the nightmare and shuddered. "I wish you'd give this up," she said under her breath.

"Stop worrying," he said with irritation.

"You might as well order me to stop breathing," she said angrily. "You enjoy daring fate to come after you. Sometimes I think you're subconsciously entertaining a death wish."

He slammed his coffee cup down. "That's ridiculous and you know it. Why the hell would I want to kill myself?"

"You want some textbook reasons? Your father treated you badly, so you thought you weren't worth much. You're lucky you didn't start abusing yourself with alcohol and drugs. Stunt work's a little more glamorous, but eventually, if you keep it up, it'll do the job."

He glared at her. "Enough of this Freudian garbage. I do stunt work because I like it. Either accept me as I am or . . ."

"Or what?" she seethed. "Get out of your life?"

"No." Dylan's voice softened. "Don't ever get out of my life. I need you, Sonia, and I love you."

"Dylan," she pleaded. "Don't you understand? I'm scared to lose you."

Chapter 14

USUALLY SONIA LOOKED FORWARD TO SEEING patients and helping them learn to cope with their problems, but this afternoon she found herself wishing she could scream, "Hey listen, you think you have troubles? Let me tell you what's going on in my life."

What was the saying, "Physician, heal thyself"? As a psychologist, she had handled things all wrong with Dylan, blowing up at him like that. But the woman in her who loved him and wanted him safe had overshadowed the professional.

He had not left her many alternatives. It was like a married man telling his wife he had a mistress, then informing her that if she didn't like it she could leave.

Maybe she should.

How could she live with that terror every time he went out on a job? It wasn't a situation that would eventually make a person callous. As she grew to love him more, her fear of losing him would only intensify. And it was no use trying to keep her feelings hidden from him. She knew what that did to people.

When Dylan arrived at her apartment that night, he was in good spirits. "I've finally come up with a solution to our dilemma."

"You've decided to take up interior decorating?" she asked hopefully.

He laughed. "No, I've thought of a way you can learn to live with my profession. What's frightening you is the unknown."

"It is?"

"When you first heard about car hits, you panicked, right? But after you saw Marlee and me do a couple of hits and understood what was involved, you relaxed."

"I wouldn't say I was exactly relaxed, but you're right, it wasn't as frightening."

He put his arm around her. "I wish there were some way I could run a reel of my life through a movie projector so you could count how many hours I've spent hanging upside down from a trapeze bar in all kinds of circumstances. To me it's as natural as sipping tea. In fact, I've spent a hell of a lot more hours in the air swinging from a trapeze than I have sipping tea."

She gave him a weak smile. "You're beginning to make sense, and that worries me."

He grinned and continued enthusiastically,

"What you have to do is come with me on a shoot and see how safely everything's handled."

She stood up abruptly, nearly knocking her chair over. "Are you out of your blazing mind?"

He was beside her in a second, his arms wrapped around her. "Would you hear me out?"

"I'm not going to watch you do that helicopter stunt. No way!"

He caressed her hair. "Watching Quinn and me work out at my house didn't give you a heart attack, did it?"

"It gave me a few jitters."

"But you saw the precautions we take. If you were to come out on a shoot, you'd know what goes on. The problem right now is you're imagining things that could never happen."

"Like your being dropped too low and hitting the pavement?"

He kissed the top of her head. "Any pilot knows how to keep his altitude steady. I'm sure that part of the dream is just some weird memory from out of my childhood that's gotten tangled up in the nightmare. It's no more apt to happen than your doing the stunt with me."

He led her into the bedroom and turned out the light. After slipping her sweater over her head, he caressed her bare shoulders, running his hands down her back.

"Sonia, I want you to get over your fear about my work. Give us that chance."

She planted soft kisses on his face while unbuttoning his shirt. "Dylan, I do want to, but watching you hang up there from a helicopter

". . . I don't know. What if it makes me even more terrified?"

"It won't. Whenever Papa Colombo had a horse that was scared of something, like rattling papers, he'd take the animal to that object, let him sniff and look at it a long time, and then if the horse was still skittish, he'd put carrots down on the papers and rattle them while the horse ate. And that cured him."

"Dylan," she murmured as she feathered kisses across his cheek, "I hate to break this to you, but feeding me carrots while I watch you do stunts isn't going to help."

"How about Thai food?"

She laughed as she undid his belt buckle. "Well, Thai food, maybe."

Dylan chuckled as he guided her down on the bed. "I'll have the Chans fix you a box lunch on the day of the filming."

He ran his hands lovingly over her breasts, and as his mouth came down on the satiny tip of one, she fell back against the pillows and let all the wondrous, fiery sensations course through her.

Maybe he was right. What could she lose by giving it a chance? And there was so much to gain.

"Dylan, Dylan," she murmured.

When he finally thrust inside her she arched to him, meeting the pounding rhythm and curling her fingers into his shoulders.

Later, as they lay breathless and sated in each other's arms, he said, "You must go on that shoot with me. It's the only way to cure you."

"It's unfair to ask me anything at this moment. Whatever you asked, I'd say yes."

"Then will you marry me?"

Tears came to her eyes, and she hugged him tighter. "Are you sure you meant that?"

"I've never been more sure of anything. I love you, Sonia. I want to spend the rest of my life with you."

"I love you, and my first reaction is to say yes, but . . . let's wait until after the shoot. I want to see if I can handle that first."

"You will, darlin', I know you will."

Two days before the shoot Dylan and Marlee came to the lab to do another experiment.

As Marlee walked into the isolation booth, Sonia noticed that she wasn't her usually bubbly, exuberant self. "I guess I'm nervous about that acting job," she admitted. "I'm so afraid I'll forget my lines and embarrass Frank. And I also feel badly about letting Dylan down."

"Come on, Marlee, he was really happy for you to get that part."

"But he's gone through two stuntwomen, and now he's trying to get a third."

"He didn't say anything to me about it," said Sonia worriedly.

"I guess he didn't want to upset you."

"Why is he having such a hard time?"

"Not many people are excited about hanging on to a guy's wrists a hundred fifty feet up in midair, I guess."

"It didn't bother you, though."

"That's because I've worked with Dylan so much on the trapeze. Once he's got ahold of you, he's like a bulldog. There's no way you're going to slip. One time I was hanging just by the fingers of one hand, but he managed to get a solid grip on me. There's nothing difficult in that stunt. All you have to do is hang on. I don't know why some of these women are so chicken. You could even do it if you wanted, Sonia."

"I think I'll pass," she joked nervously.

"I understand you're going out to watch the filming."

"I told Dylan I would, but now I'm having second thoughts."

"Don't be silly. Just be sure to take a deck of cards."

"For what?"

"To play. There's nothing more boring than movie making. They spend hours adjusting the lights and taking the same scene over and over from different angles. You'll be bored to tears."

"You don't think watching the stunt will be scary?"

"Watching Dylan do a stunt is like watching Baryshnikov do ballet. He raises it up to an art form. Besides that, he's a pro, one of the most respected stuntmen in the business. He doesn't bitch and moan about every little thing; he just goes in and gets the job done. Just be sure you take cards. It probably won't take very long for that shot, and then you'll have to hang around the rest of the day."

"Whatever for?"

"Union thing. It's really dumb. Movie sets are full of bored people just waiting to clock out or collect an extra meal penalty."

Marlee's comments about being bored let Sonia breathe easier, but she was more nervous than ever about Dylan's not being able to find a stuntwoman to go up there with him.

When she went over the charts at the end of the experiment, she discovered there had been only one instance of ESP and none of precognition. It was the lowest score Dylan and Marlee had ever had. She wondered if emotional factors could have entered into it. Both of them were distracted.

"Pretty potent stuff, your hypnosis," he joked with her that night. "If I were a smoker, I'd have you hypnotize me to quit. What a shame I don't have any more bad habits you could rid me of."

"What about stunt work?"

He gave her a playful hug. "Not on your life."

She ran her finger around the back of his neck. "Marlee said you were having a hard time finding a stuntwoman."

"I've far from exhausted the supply."

"But what if you don't find anyone? Would they cancel it?"

"Someone will turn up."

"You only have a few days left."

"I keep telling you, don't worry about it."

The night before the shoot Sonia and Dylan went to the Thai restaurant for dinner. He was in such high spirits he decided they should walk the two miles. Sonia was glad to comply, hoping the vigorous walk would work off some of her anxiety. It was a clear night, the stars twinkling overhead, fragrances of spring in the air as they passed open fields of wild mustard, anise and lilac.

Dylan laughed and joked with the Chans and ordered so many dishes they could barely finish all the food.

He told her he was pleased with the stunt-woman he'd finally found, but Sonia suspected that he didn't have much confidence in her. It was impossible to know what his true feelings were, for if he had any reservations about the stunt tomorrow, he was keeping silent about them. And she did the same.

"Are there any special exercises you do to prepare yourself just before doing a stunt?" she asked him on the way home.

"Pray."

"Are you kidding?"

"It's said there are no atheists in a foxhole. Not many in the circus or in stunt work either."

It was the first time he'd mentioned this spiritual side of him. "Did you have a religious up-bringing?"

"Not until I left my father. With the Colombos it was unavoidable. At first I resented it, but later, especially when I was in Vietnam, I was grateful. What about you?"

"My parents made me go to a Sunday school, but they were rather lackadaisical about the rest. I found out later that my father was a confirmed atheist. Sometimes I wish my faith were stronger."

"Like now?"

"Yes." She squeezed his hand.

"I feel good about everything, Sonia. Maybe it's love and springtime, but there haven't been any more nightmares. It's strange to feel happy and peaceful and ready to conquer the world all at once."

She wished she could say the same. All she felt was an anxious, churning fear that never seemed to leave her. It had even begun to overshadow the certainty of her love for Dylan.

He might not be plagued with any more nightmares, but now she was. They were strangely surreal dreams that kept harping back to her little brother. The situations changed, but always climaxed with his being in danger and her unable to help him.

Dylan slept soundly again that night, while she remained awake, trying to keep still so as not to disturb his sleep. He needed all the rest he could get to be sharp in the morning, and she was glad the hypnosis had helped him in that respect.

The digital clock by the bed changed numbers with annoying regularity. If only there were a way to freeze time so that she could keep Dylan safe and warm beside her in bed.

Just as Quinn had once said, Dylan awoke moments before the alarm actually went off. He pulled her close and kissed her in his sleepy way. "This is the fun side of the movie business—getting up at the crack of dawn. Come on, we'll take a shower together. It'll make it easier."

She stood passively as he soaped her up, letting the water flow onto her body. Some of the numbness of a sleepless night was leaving as she became aroused by his soapy caresses.

Before she knew it, they were sharing wet kisses and she was leaning up against the shower stall while he made love to her. It did wonders for her outlook.

"What a way to start the day," she murmured with a silly smile as he rubbed her dry with a thick towel. "Don't let this secret out or the instant-coffee people will go out of business."

Though she hadn't been able to sleep at all the night before, she drifted off easily in the front seat of the Cobra on the long drive out to the desert location.

When they arrived, she was amazed at the number of cars, vans, trucks and mobile dressing rooms. The helicopter was also there, and she regarded it with shuddering distrust. Dylan quickly found her a canvas folding chair and a cup of coffee and told her to enjoy what was going on while he got things set up.

She glanced around and decided that Marlee might have been right. A lot of people seemed to be just standing or sitting around doing nothing in particular but drinking coffee. The only peo-

ple who looked legitimately busy were techni-
cians who were moving cables and setting up
lights.

Dylan was over by the helicopter talking to
several men and a woman. They all seemed to
be hitting it off, laughing and joking. At least
they weren't nervous. A good sign, she thought.
All morning, she would be looking for good
signs. She was as bad as a soothsayer studying
the entrails of sheep.

It seemed like hours before the actual shooting
got under way. She hadn't realized that Dylan
would be doing anything more than the stunt
he'd talked about, so she was surprised to see
him run through some explosions, duck under
whipping helicopter blades, and leap inside just
as it began to lift off.

There were four takes, and during each one
her heart stopped and she gripped the arms of
her folding chair with all her might. She already
knew he had been wrong to insist she come. If
she was this terrified now, how would she be
watching him hang upside down from that helicopter?

In between takes, he came over and brought
her another cup of coffee and a donut. He was
feeling good about the way the scene had come
off, and she did her best to hide her real feelings.
There was no reason to burden him with her
fears about the big one still ahead; he had
enough to think about.

"You see? There was nothing scary about
that," he said confidently.

"It was interesting." She feigned an indifferent shrug. "Marlee was right, though. Between takes it's really very dull. I thought at least there'd be a balding director in jodhpurs with a megaphone."

Dylan laughed. "That's the director over there."

"I know, but he has long hair, is wearing jeans, and looks about sixteen."

"The theory in Hollywood is that if you don't have a juvenile director, the movie won't appeal to juvenile audiences who spend the money at the box office."

"I'd think directing a movie would be kind of fun. You ever considered it?"

"I could probably do as well as any of these guys with the action stuff, but I don't know the first thing about drama. One of these days what I'll do is become a stunt coordinator."

"Then you wouldn't actually have to do the stunts?"

He gave her a kiss on the cheek. "You'd like that, wouldn't you?"

"I won't deny it." She glanced over at the helicopter pilot, who was chatting with the stuntwoman. "You seem to have a nice rapport with the helicopter pilot."

"He's a nice enough guy, but his timing's a little off. I nearly didn't make that last leap into the chopper, he took off so fast."

Despite her efforts to conceal it, the fear must have shown vividly on her face, for he threw a reassuring arm around her shoulders. "Don't worry about the big one. I've had a long talk with him and he understands what he has to do."

While they waited for the cameras to set up for the next shot, Dylan explained what was going on. "When you see a film, you really only think about what's on the screen," she said. "I don't know that I'll ever be able to see another movie without thinking about all these hordes of people lounging around with their paper coffee cups."

The stunt coordinator came up to them and suggested Dylan change into the clothes he was going to be wearing in the scene, as they were almost ready to begin.

Dylan kissed Sonia lightly and whispered, "See you later, honey. Don't forget I love you."

A terrible fear shot through the pit of her stomach that those would be the last words she'd ever hear him say.

Was that queasy feeling a premonition? Just because she'd never had one didn't mean she was incapable. Many of the reports she'd read were of people who'd never had a psychic experience in their lives. Strong emotions were usually the catalyst.

She hoped what she felt was nothing more than an expected dose of fear heightened by a vivid imagination.

Dylan came out of the dressing room in black slacks and a black turtleneck, the clothes the movie's superspy hero was wearing. Sonia caught her breath. He looked better than the star. More than one woman on the set sat up straighter.

After another conference with the director, the driver and another man got in the front seat of the red convertible, the stuntwoman in back. Dylan and the pilot climbed into the helicopter and began their ascent.

Sonia could barely breathe as she watched the helicopter climb higher and higher. The cameras and every eye on the set were focused on it. At what must have been a hundred fifty feet, the cable ladder dropped and Dylan began climbing down it.

He had been wrong about wanting her to watch. This was much worse than she could have imagined. As she watched the ladder sway back and forth, she thought of every horrible thing that could go wrong—a broken rung, a strong gust of wind. Only one misstep and he would plummet to the ground. Nobody could survive a fall like that.

She wanted to hide her eyes but found she couldn't. He was on the last rung, down to the trapeze bar. She remembered his reassurances, all the hours he'd spent on a trapeze. This is nothing for him, she told herself, just another job.

The red convertible was cued to begin driving down the highway, and as the helicopter hovered over the car, Dylan hung upside down from the trapeze bar.

But the car and helicopter were not keeping a

steady pace. One moment the car would shoot slightly ahead, and the next, the helicopter. Just when she was beginning to despair of their ever coming into line, they did and it was the cue for the chopper to drop lower.

Dylan's arms were extended and the stunt-woman's hands reached up for his. Then suddenly the chopper dropped even lower. Sonia saw Dylan kick the trapeze bar loose and fall headfirst into the back seat of the convertible.

She held her breath until he resurfaced. The helicopter made a landing and they had another conference. Although she was some distance from them, Sonia could see by Dylan's gestures that he was furious at the pilot.

Was he refusing to go ahead with the stunt now? She prayed it was the case. He had made it through one take with only a minor mishap. Why couldn't he leave now?

Fear clamped around her chest like a vise as she saw him climb back into the helicopter.

Be optimistic, she told herself. That was a rehearsal. The pilot knows now what he did wrong and he'll get it right this time. She relaxed slightly when she saw that the car had slowed down considerably and the helicopter did not climb up quite so high.

Dylan started down the ladder again, but this time he did not remain sitting on the trapeze bar for very long. He hung from his knees upside down almost immediately as the helicopter continued to go lower.

She silently cursed the director, who must have requested the change. That had to be infinitely more dangerous! At least this time there seemed to be no coordination problems. The driver and pilot were keeping the same speed.

In fact, to her surprise, everything was going smoothly. The stuntwoman reached her hands up, clasped Dylan's wrists, and the helicopter began to rise with them both. Then suddenly the woman let go and dropped back down into the car.

Someone standing beside Sonia said, "I think she chickened out at the last minute."

"I wouldn't have waited that long," said another.

Sonia gave the stuntwoman the benefit of the doubt. Perhaps she hadn't been able to get a tight enough grip. Waiting until you were hanging a hundred fifty feet up was no time to have second thoughts about slipping.

Dylan climbed back up the ladder and into the helicopter. The red convertible was brought back to its starting point and cued again.

Sonia steeled herself, but for the first time she began to think Dylan might have been wise in letting her see the stunt. Her heart was still racing, but at least it wasn't skipping beats and she was no longer clutching at the arms of the chair.

As the helicopter hovered over the car, Dylan came down the ladder again and onto the trapeze bar. The stuntwoman was reaching up, nearly touching Dylan's hands.

Then for no apparent reason the helicopter veered to the left. It was no longer directly over the back seat of the car and it was dropping lower. Dylan was hitting the side of the car. His head was level with the spinning back wheel of the car.

Sonia felt faint. She knew what would happen next. His head slammed into the pavement.

Chapter 15

SONIA WAS SCREAMING, HER VOICE SOUNDING FAR away, as though it were coming from the end of a long tunnel. Other voices were echoing the screams. Sharp, stabbing lights burst in her head. She was dizzy, nauseous, faint; then everything went black.

When she came to, she was in one of the trailers and a uniformed nurse was standing over her. Immediately, Sonia wished for oblivion again. Sobs wracked her body as she thought about Dylan. "I couldn't help him," she said in choked gusts. "There was nothing I could do to help him. And now it's too late. I should have talked him out of it somehow."

The trailer door opened and she gasped. Why was she frightened? She was the gypsy lady who dealt in ghosts and disembodied spirits, and this was obviously one staring at her. Dylan had to have been killed. Nobody could hit the pavement with that impact and live. Yet he looked very solid and alive as he rushed toward her.

"Dylan?"

"I heard you fainted. You all right, darlin'?"

His arms were around her and she hugged him as tight as she could, grateful he was no apparition.

"Thank God, Dylan, thank God. I thought you were. . . ."

"It'll take more than that to kill me," he said softly.

She pushed him away from her for a moment and simply feasted her eyes. There were a few cuts and bruises, torn clothes. But he was in one piece. "Not even any broken bones?"

"Not a one."

"But how did you manage to come out of that?"

"I kicked loose and kept rolling on the pavement so the shock of impact would be evenly distributed."

She wrapped her arms around his neck and covered his dusty face with kisses. "How clever you are."

He chuckled softly. "That's what I've been telling you. This is my business."

He pried himself loose from her arms. "As long as you're okay, I'd better get back. I've got to get changed for another take."

She paled. "No—Dylan, you're not going up there again."

"Of course I am. They still haven't gotten the shot."

She shook with rage and desperation. "That pilot is a maniac. He'll kill you! Dylan, listen to me. It's not that important. It's only a movie. If they don't have that scene, they'll write something else. You've done your duty. Please, please, don't go back up there."

Tears were running down her face, and she tried in vain to wipe them away as she spoke. She'd had one reprieve with him. Would she be lucky enough to have another?

"I've got to do it," he said quietly. He started to kiss her, but she shrugged him off.

"I won't watch this one, Dylan—I'll never watch one again. After this I never want to see you again. I won't go through this. You said my imagination would be worse, but it couldn't be."

"Sonia . . ."

Desperate, she'd try anything. "There was your dream. It all happened just like in the nightmare, remember? Isn't that proof enough it was a warning to you?"

"Okay, it happened like in the nightmare. It must have been a premonition, but now it's over. Nothing is going to happen on the next take. We'll have it wrapped up in a half hour, and then I'll come back here and take you home."

Sonia had seen enough hysterical people to know that she was on the verge of it. "You talk about love, but it's only on your terms," she said shakily. "When it was between doing your hypnosis and my research, I didn't hesitate to put you first. Your well-being was the only thing I considered. But I can see that doesn't work both ways. I'm given no choice but to accept your doing these awful stunts. My feelings don't mean anything to you."

"Sonia, honey, that's not true—"

"Then how can you go back out there?"

"Let's talk about this tonight. Right now I've got to go finish up that stunt." He turned toward the nurse. "Why don't you give her a sedative. I'll be back in a little while."

"You walk out that door and you will never see me again!"

"Tonight, Sonia, we'll get it all straightened out."

After the door closed, she sank back down on the cot and clenched her teeth to hold back the tears.

"Would you like a tranquilizer?" the nurse asked politely.

"The best tranquilizer is for me to get out of Dylan Hamlin's life."

"That's the way with most men," said the nurse sympathetically. "Their work always comes before their women."

"Not this woman," Sonia said with trembling vehemence. "I'm through following the Pied Piper. If he's bent on self-destruction, he can count me out as witness. Do you suppose there's anyone driving back into town soon?"

"Probably," said the nurse. "People are coming and going all day. I'll ask around."

She returned a few minutes later with the news that someone from wardrobe was going into Burbank. "Is that close to where you want to go?"

"No, but I can call a taxi from there. Thanks a million. Sorry to have caused you any inconvenience."

The nurse smiled. "That's what I'm here for. And hey, I admire you for what you said. I hope you stick to your guns. Most of us gals simply put up with whatever those selfish bastards dish out."

As the car pulled out, Sonia stole a glance in the direction of the helicopter. Dylan was once again descending the ladder. She brushed a tear from her cheek and forced her eyes away.

"You came out here with Dylan Hamlin, didn't you?" asked the woman driving the car.

"Yes." Sonia was curt. She really would prefer silence on the long drive back to the city.

"He's got a lot of guts. I'll hand him that."

Sonia didn't answer, hoping it would put an end to the subject.

"I had a boyfriend who was a stuntman once," the young woman continued. "The guy couldn't stand still for a minute. They're like that. Get a bunch of them together and they're punching each other, throwing judo flips, karate chops. It's like they have to be constantly in motion. I don't know about Hamlin; he seems pretty laid back. But some of the guys seem to have all this violence seething just under the surface."

Sonia had just about had enough. The psychological makeup of the average stuntman was not a subject she wanted to discuss. "I'll bet you've had some fascinating experiences with big stars, working in the wardrobe department," she said brightly.

"Oh, have I!"

Sonia congratulated herself on a wise choice of topics. With the right question interjected here and there, Sonia kept the woman going on the idiosyncrasies of Hollywood stars all the way into Burbank.

Leaving the set, however, didn't lessen her anxiety. A second didn't go by that she didn't worry if he'd made it through the last take alive. And if he made it alive, had he been injured? At any moment she expected to see an ambulance whizzing by them.

It was after six by the time the taxi dropped her off in front of her apartment. She debated going to the store to pick up something for dinner, then decided against it. The way her insides were churning, she couldn't eat.

Instead, she went in and poured herself a glass of chilled Chablis, took it with her into the bathtub and sipped it slowly while she soaked in the hot water and bubbles.

The telephone was ringing in the other room. Let it ring off the hook, she fumed, and sank down further in the water. She didn't want to talk to anyone, least of all Dylan if by some miracle he'd managed to survive.

When the water went tepid and the glass of Chablis was finished, she stepped out of the tub. The phone was ringing again. She counted twelve rings before the caller hung up.

Since she'd had no sleep the night before, the

wine made her sleepy, but just as she climbed into bed the phone rang again. If that kept up she'd never get any sleep.

Pulling herself up, she went into the kitchen, took the phone off the hook, then returned to bed. But tired as she was, sleep still wouldn't come. Helicopter blades were whipping around in her brain, and scenes of the stunt kept drifting into her consciousness.

Finally, in desperation, she went into the kitchen to fix some herb tea. She had just finished pouring a cup when the doorbell rang.

"It's me," Dylan shouted. "Dammit, let me in!"

Afraid he'd wake up the neighbors, she reluctantly went to the door. Without opening it, she said icily, "I said I never wanted to see you again and I meant it."

"Sonia, open the door so we can at least talk face-to-face."

"It's not getting through to you. I never want to see your face again. Go away!"

"I've broken down doors stronger than this."

He was certainly capable and angry enough to do it. Feeling defeated, she opened the door.

He stormed in. "What the hell did you mean by leaving there today?"

"Do I have to spell it out for you?" she said sarcastically, and went back to her tea on the kitchen counter.

His eyes raked over the soft curves of her body visible under the deep burgundy negligee. "Come here, gypsy lady."

"Tea?" She primly poured him a cup. "Oh,

that's right, you'd rather hang upside down from a trapeze bar than sip tea."

He took the cup and followed her to the dining room table. "Sonia, I had to finish that stunt today."

"I could have said the same thing about my experiments in precognition, but if you recall, I didn't beg you to indulge me."

Dylan took a sip of the tea and winced. "What the hell is this?"

"Chamomile tea."

"No wonder I prefer hanging from a trapeze bar. You got anything stronger than this?"

There were some liquor bottles on the buffet. "Help yourself," she said.

Dylan rose and poured himself a snifter of brandy.

"I'll take one too," she said with a sigh. Facing Dylan Hamlin took something stronger than herb tea. Remembering the nurse's parting words, she was determined to stick to her guns.

"All right, maybe it was selfish. But when I start something, I finish it. I've never backed out of any stunt and I wasn't going to begin today. It was a matter of pride."

"Macho garbage," she muttered.

"Call it what you will, but I had to do it."

"You were afraid your cronies would think you were a coward, but I'll bet not one of them would have gotten up there on that trapeze bar. What matters is that my feelings didn't figure in your thinking at all."

"That's not true. Your feelings are everything to me. Dammit, Sonia, I want to marry you."

Her dark eyes blazed with unbridled anger. "You made your decision about our marriage when you chose that stunt over me. It's ironic. I was always afraid that if I gave my love to a man, something disastrous would happen. Well, it nearly did today, and the odds of its happening if you continue in that line of work are pretty good. You may enjoy betting on long shots, but I'm not a gambler. Like I told you once before, I know my limits. Do you know how close I was to hysteria today? I went that route when I was a child, and I have no intention of going back to that hell. Yet that's all I'd have to look forward to as your wife. Forget it, Dylan."

He reached across the table and caressed her bare shoulder. "That's what I'm trying to tell you, my love. That stunt was my last. I'm giving it up."

"You are?" She felt a little foolish after her long tirade.

"Come here and sit on my lap. You're too far away." This time she complied and felt a warm glow as he wrapped his strong arms around her. "My God, this is a sexy thing." He touched the gauzy nightgown. "How come you never wore this around me before?"

"I've never worn any nightgown around you before. Dylan, have you really decided to give up stunt work?"

"Well, not exactly."

She stiffened. "What's that supposed to mean?"

"From now on I'm going to be a stunt coordinator. When I saw your face back there in the first-aid trailer, it was like a shot of *déjà vu* until I realized where I'd seen you looking that terrified before. It was in the nightmare. But it wasn't my father who was making you suffer this time; it was me. Sonia, you're all that matters to me."

She buried her face in his neck. "Now you make me feel awful about taking you away from something you love."

"You're what I love. Stunt work has been good, I won't deny it. But I'm getting close to forty. That doesn't leave too many years left in this business. It's too demanding physically. The bruises I got today won't heal as fast as they used to. Maybe that crack on the pavement knocked some sense into my head."

She brushed her lips over his cheek and found his mouth, kissing him hungrily. "It's a shame you can't see into the future anymore," she mused. "I wonder what it will bring us."

"Happiness, a couple of kids—a girl first, then a boy—a golden retriever and a blue station wagon."

She sat back and gazed at him with surprise. "That's pretty specific."

"My premonitions usually are."

"But I thought. . . ."

"I wouldn't have stormed in here tonight if I weren't absolutely sure."

"But the hypnosis."

"Remind me never to go to you if I have to quit smoking."

"It didn't work?"

He held her face and kissed her lightly on the nose. "Not entirely, darlin'. Last night I had the dream again about the stunt. This one was accurate down to the correct pilot and stuntwoman. Neither you nor my father was in it."

"But you didn't wake up screaming. I would have known. I was awake all night."

He pulled her close and ran his hands lovingly over her back. "Remember the part of the hypnosis where you said I'd still have the dreams, but I wouldn't remember them and they wouldn't disturb me? Well, only part of that worked. I still had the dream and I remembered it, only it didn't disturb me. I knew there'd be trouble but that I was going to come out of it okay. I think the reason my ESP didn't work in the lab the other day was that Marlee's attention was all blocked up with nervousness about her part in the TV series. You can tell McCabe we'll go on with the experiments as soon as you want."

She touched his face and said softly, "And when did you have the one about the kids and the station wagon?"

"When we were driving out to the desert this morning and you were sleeping, I reached over and held your hand."

"But what if I decide I want a red station wagon?"

"We'll get a green polka dot one if we feel like it."

"But if you already saw it, do you really think we have a choice?"

He hugged her tighter. "We can do anything we damn well please. Everyone controls his own fate. Sometimes we do it through dreams and sometimes it's just the minute-to-minute decisions that make up our lives. Any soothsayer worth his salt will tell you that."

Afterword

ALTHOUGH THE ESP EXPERIMENTS IN THIS BOOK are of my own invention, they are based on those conducted by psychologist Dr. Thelma Moss, a charming, spellbinding lady. My thanks to the gracious library staff at the Neuropsychiatric Institute at UCLA for allowing me access to Dr. Moss's papers and their parapsychology files.

There is not enough space to thank all the stuntpeople who helped me, an astonishing number of whom related psychic experiences connected with their work. But I must mention Instant Action Coordinators, and the Kahana Stunt School in Chatsworth, California, who were extremely helpful. Stuntwoman Debbie Kahana gave me invaluable insights into her profession. It's to the extraordinary stuntman and former trapeze flyer Bob Yerkes that I owe the description of that harrowing helicopter stunt. Yes, it did happen with all the blunders. I watched a videotape of those takes. It's also to Bob that I owe a delightful afternoon in his backyard watching rehearsals for the *Circus of the Stars*.

WIN

a fabulous $50,000 diamond jewelry collection

ENTER

by filling out the coupon below and mailing it by September 30, 1985

Send entries to:

U.S.
Silhouette Diamond Sweepstakes
P.O. Box 779
Madison Square Station
New York, NY 10159

Canada
Silhouette Diamond Sweepstakes
Suite 191
238 Davenport Road
Toronto, Ontario M5R 1J6

SILHOUETTE DIAMOND SWEEPSTAKES
ENTRY FORM

☐ Mrs.   ☐ Miss   ☐ Ms   ☐ Mr.

NAME _____ (please print)

ADDRESS _____ APT. #

CITY _____

STATE/(PROV.) _____

ZIP/(POSTAL CODE) _____

RTD-A-1

RULES FOR SILHOUETTE DIAMOND SWEEPSTAKES

OFFICIAL RULES—NO PURCHASE NECESSARY

1. Silhouette Diamond Sweepstakes is open to Canadian (except Quebec) and United States residents 18 years or older at the time of entry. Employees and immediate families of the publishers of Silhouette, their affiliates, retailers, distributors, printers, agencies and RONALD SMILEY INC. are excluded.

2. To enter, print your name and address on the official entry form or on a 3" x 5" slip of paper. You may enter as often as you choose, but each envelope must contain only one entry. Mail entries first class in Canada to Silhouette Diamond Sweepstakes, Suite 191, 238 Davenport Road, Toronto, Ontario M5R 1J6. In the United States, mail to Silhouette Diamond Sweepstakes, P.O. Box 779, Madison Square Station, New York, NY 10159. Entries must be postmarked between February 1 and September 30, 1985. Silhouette is not responsible for lost, late or misdirected mail.

3. First Prize of diamond jewelry, consisting of a necklace, ring, bracelet and earrings will be awarded. Approximate retail value is $50,000 U.S./$62,500 Canadian. Second Prize of 100 Silhouette Home Reader Service Subscriptions will be awarded. Approximate retail value of each is $162.00 U.S./$180.00 Canadian. No substitution, duplication, cash redemption or transfer of prizes will be permitted. Odds of winning depend upon the number of valid entries received. One prize to a family or household. Income taxes, other taxes and insurance on First Prize are the sole responsibility of the winners.

4. Winners will be selected under the supervision of RONALD SMILEY INC., an independent judging organization whose decisions are final, by random drawings from valid entries postmarked by September 30, 1985, and received no later than October 7, 1985. Entry in this sweepstakes indicates your awareness of the Official Rules. Winners who are residents of Canada must answer correctly a time-related arithmetical skill-testing question to qualify. First Prize winner will be notified by certified mail and must submit an Affidavit of Compliance within 10 days of notification. Returned Affidavits or prizes that are refused or undeliverable will result in alternative names being randomly drawn. Winners may be asked for use of their name and photo at no additional compensation.

5. For a First Prize winner list, send a stamped self-addressed envelope postmarked by September 30, 1985. In Canada, mail to Silhouette Diamond Contest Winner, Suite 309, 238 Davenport Road, Toronto, Ontario M5R 1J6. In the United States, mail to Silhouette Diamond Contest Winner, P.O. Box 182, Bowling Green Station, New York, NY 10274. This offer will appear in Silhouette publications and at participating retailers. Offer void in Quebec and subject to all Federal, Provincial, State and Municipal laws and regulations and wherever prohibited or restricted by law.

SDR-A-1

READERS' COMMENTS ON
SILHOUETTE INTIMATE MOMENTS:

"About a month ago a friend loaned me my first Silhouette. I was thoroughly surprised as well as totally addicted. Last week I read a Silhouette Intimate Moments and I was even more pleased. They are the best romance series novels I have ever read. They give much more depth to the plot, characters, and the story is fundamentally realistic. They incorporate tasteful sex scenes, which is a must, especially in the 1980's. I only hope you can publish them fast enough."

S.B.*, Lees Summit, MO

"After noticing the attractive covers on the new line of Silhouette Intimate Moments, I decided to read the inside and discovered that this new line was more in the line of books that I like to read. I do want to say I enjoyed the books because they are so realistic and a lot more truthful than so many romance books today."

J.C., Onekama, MI

"I would like to compliment you on your books. I will continue to purchase all of the Silhouette Intimate Moments. They are your best line of books that I have had the pleasure of reading."

S.M., Billings, MT

*names available on request